THE SCARLET
LETTER STORM

THE SCARLET LETTER STORM

MARY T. McCARTHY

Copyright © 2016 by Mary T. McCarthy
Cover and jacket design by Georgia Morrissey
Interior design by E.M. Tippetts Book Designs

ISBN 978-1-940610-90-0
eISBN: 978-1-943818-13-6

First Trade Paperback edition: May 2016
by Polis Books, LLC

1201 Hudson Street
Hoboken, NJ 07030
www.PolisBooks.com

POLIS BOOKS

Other books by

MARY T. McCARTHY

The Scarlet Letter Society
The Scarlet Letter Scandal

For Kara
and for Tilghman Island,
my muses

Prologue

April 2011

Lisa Swain walked into Zoomdweebies Coffee Shop in historic downtown Keytown, Maryland, on this chilly spring morning before heading one block over to open her bakery. She greeted the owner, Zarina, as she always did. Once again she noticed the two women at their usual table in the corner.

"The usual?" asked Zarina.

"Sure," said Lisa. "Too early in the morning to be adventurous! But I will try one of those blueberry scones."

"Just baked them this morning," said Zarina.

"Even though I have a bakery, it's always nice to start off the morning with something baked by someone else," said Lisa.

"Let me warm it up for you with some butter and I'll bring it over, if you have a second to sit down," said Zarina. She looked over at the table where Maggie and Eva were sitting.

Lisa too glanced quickly over at the seated women.

"Sure," she said. "Thanks, Zarina."

Lisa felt guilty for doing it, but once again she took the table beside the two women. She had seen them about a half a dozen times or so in the coffee shop: the auburn-haired woman she recognized as owning the Wings Vintage Clothing store in town, and the black-haired, well-dressed woman. She knew their names from eavesdropping on their conversations: Maggie and Eva. There used to be a third woman in the group, Stacy, with a long blond braid, but Lisa knew she'd moved away from town a few months before.

Zarina brought over a caramel latte and blueberry scone, and Lisa thanked her. Lisa had her journal out and was writing in it. Her journal was her shield — when she wrote in it, she didn't have to talk to anyone, but also it seemed to make her invisible, or she liked to pretend it did. The women at the next table wouldn't notice she was eavesdropping on them if she was writing away in a journal, minding her own business. So she wrote, but they didn't know she was writing about them and their club, the Scarlet Letter Society.

"If I have to live another moment in this marriage with Joe, I will hurl myself off that bay bridge the next time I cross it to visit my mother's cottage," said Eva.

"Well, you damn well aren't coming to me for marriage advice after I just escaped my second one," said Maggie, "after cheating on both my husbands."

"Thank God for lovers," said Eva. "Or how the hell would we stay married to anyone in the first place?"

"It's a fair question, friend," said Maggie.

Lisa scribbled furiously. She was miserable in her marriage, too. She had no friends in the subdivision, Stony Mill, where she lived, and she had decided she wanted to be friends with Maggie and Eva. Her problem was that she was painfully shy, so she didn't know how to approach them. Her other problem was that she wasn't cheating on her husband, which seemed to be the singular requirement for membership in the Scarlet Letter Society. Her only advantage, really, was that "society" seemed to be a group word, and right now there were only two of them, so they were down a member. One day, she was just going to do it — somehow figure out a way to approach them. She finished her scone and coffee, closed her journal, thanked Zarina, and left, heading over to her bakery a block away.

Less than an hour later, Lisa was at her bakery, Blackbirds Pie, rolling out dough on the counter when she heard the gentle ting-a-ling *of the shop door. She couldn't believe her eyes. Standing before her were Maggie and Eva, holding coffees.*

She tried to hide the shock from her face. This was her chance. Lisa stood up, smoothing down her tan skirt, pulling her blond ponytail tighter. It gave her confidence that she was blond — maybe she could fill the blond contingent in the group. She walked up to the counter.

"Welcome to Blackbirds Pie Bakery," said Lisa. "May I help you?"

"Yeah," said Maggie, "our friend Zarina said we had to try the chocolate croissants over here so we wanted to get two of those to go."

"I was just at Zarina's shop today too!" she said, putting croissants in individual bags, placing them on the counter. "First ones are on the house."

Then Lisa started speaking very quickly. "Listen, you ladies don't know me, and this is a little bit awkward, but my name is Lisa. I'm sure it's very rude that I overheard your coffee shop conversation, but I just want you to know that um, I'm cheating on my husband and I need a club and I wondered if you might consider..."

Maggie started laughing. Eva looked at Lisa like she was from another planet.

"Hello, there, Lisa the baker," said Maggie, "who is cheating on her husband. That's a pretty brave move, just putting that out there like that."

"I think 'rude' is the word she used," said Eva, the corporate attorney. "She was listening in on our conversations without permission for who knows what period of time..."

"I'm really very sorry," said Lisa. "I would completely understand if you just told me to..."

"Aw, give the girl a break, Eva," said Maggie, looking pointedly at Eva. "That took a lot of guts. And you know what we say about the Scarlet Letter Society. It's a region where other women dare not tread."

Eva clearly struggled to hold her emotions in check, pursing her lips.

"Maybe you could join us for coffee sometime, Lisa," said Eva.

"Really?" said Lisa. "Oh, wow, thank you. That's so nice of you. I don't have anyone to talk to and I thought if I could get your advice..."

Maggie seemed to sense it was time to get Eva out of there if this was going to work.

"Yes, great," said Maggie, taking Lisa's business card and the two bakery bags. "I've got your email address here. Thanks for the croissants. We will see you at the next Scarlet Letter Society meeting. But whatever you do, don't speak of it to anyone."

"The first rule of..." began Lisa.

"Yes," said Maggie, smiling, as she and Eva turned to leave. "That."

Chapter 1

"Zoom in on her red lipstick and the ball gag," said Jo.

"Who doesn't love a good lipstick-and-ball-gag shot?" asked Zarina with a laugh.

The two women sat in a small glass room perched above the filming set floor. The old building had once served as a seafood warehouse, with thousands of pounds of crabs and oysters moving through these walls each year on Matthew's Island, tucked away in the Chesapeake Bay on Maryland's Eastern Shore. Now, the property had a sign outside reading "VXD Enterprises." Shellfish still came and went from these parts, but not from this building anymore.

Vixenden.club was a high-end sexy fantasy website for women, secretly owned and operated by schoolteacher Jo Bird and coffee shop owner Zarina Harandi, unbeknownst to most of the people in their lives.

The producer next to them gave a thumbs-up, and the director below made an "OK" hand gesture signifying he'd received the message from the studio. The screen in the studio reflected the change: the scarlet-red-lipstick-clad mouth of the actress now glistened in the shot, perched as it was around a specially-ordered black rubber ball gag. The original red ball gag hadn't looked good in any of the combinations with red lipstick, so Jo ordered the scene to be shot again. The close-up was going to be used as the main image for the short film.

"Are you happy with it?" asked Zarina, pointing toward the screen. She knew how much effort had gone into the shot.

"Yeah, I think there is just enough glitter in that deeper shade of red," said Jo, concentrating on the image before her. "Let me see the still."

The producer paused the shot, and Jo nodded. Only Zarina noticed the simultaneous exhales of the producer, the director, the makeup artist, and the photographer. Even the actresses on the set breathed quiet sighs of relief — *that crazy OCD bitch finally had the shot she wanted.*

"Pause the action and send in the photog," said the producer into his headset microphone. The director said "copy that" with the slightest hint of relief in his voice as the auburn-haired photographer made her way onto the set to capture the image that would be used on the website's main page.

"We should toast to that!" said Zarina. "This is going to be our biggest hit yet."

"It's a good feeling," said Jo. "Taking our tiny company from a crazy idea in a writing class to this secret online empire!"

She cranked up the volume on her phone and the wireless speaker in the studio blared Salt-N-Pepa's "Shoop."

The second line on the sign outside the door to VXD Enterprises read "Photography ~ Graphic Arts ~ Web Design" and most islanders had ignored the comings and goings from the building. The owner had been happy to lease the empty building. Locals figured some chicken-necker weekenders with more money than brains had set up some kind of fancy Internet business; they really couldn't care less. Though the seafood business wasn't what it used to be, hard-working watermen and their families continued season after season to bring in the shellfish for which the region was known internationally.

"The lighting is so perfect," said Zarina, looking at the small screen on the camera handed to her and Jo by the photographer.

Jo turned the sound down a few notches. *"Don't know how you do the voodoo that you do..."*

"The way the sun comes through those wooden slats— you could never capture that with electric lighting," added Zarina.

"Fantastic," said Jo. "Let's work it up with a title."

"Tara's Secret," said Zarina. "Wait until the website members see this one!"

Vixenden.club was an exclusive, members-only website for women. Its creators took great care to avoid the use of the word "pornography," which had negative connotations of male-dominated, anti-feminist '80s VHS tapes in seedy video stores. Those days were over. This brand of sex for women was on an entirely different level. This was highly specialized, professionally produced erotica for the web: steamy short stories, artfully filmed short movies, and galleries of provocative, sexy images designed for powerful, sexually high-charged, discriminating women who were willing to pay.

"We are on track to double our membership from half a million to a cool million," said Jo. "And then it looks like my days as a schoolteacher are over. Besides, if any of the island mommies figured out that their kid's elementary schoolteacher was moonlighting as an online sex empire goddess, they might object."

"True!" said Zarina, laughing. "I think people who know me as the friendly neighborhood coffee shop owner would be a little shocked, too. My mom the college professor, for instance. Though I honestly don't think she would mind. Especially if she knew I was starting to make money."

"What does your husband have to say?" asked Jo, who at thirty-four vowed to be perpetually single.

"Stanley couldn't be more laid back," said Zarina. "He calls himself a 'product tester' and always offers to check out our new stuff first! I just wish the hours at Zoomdweebies weren't so long so I could be here on the island more—but having an Internet business works out."

"I'm at the point where I hate going across that drawbridge at all," said Jo. "The phone signal on the island is terrible, but I think I'll be sad when the new cell tower starts working. I didn't want to talk to anyone on the phone that badly anyway."

"Definitely has its charms," said Zarina. "Something to be said for unplugging. Though there is some irony in the fact that we started an Internet company on an island where there's hardly enough bandwidth for four people to play Words With Friends at the same time. Ha! Well, for now I'm headed back up the road."

"I'm having lunch with Eva," said Jo. "Do you think it would be cool to talk to her about VXD Enterprises? We could really use a legal opinion on our expansion."

"I think it'd be great," said Zarina. "She will be totally cool with it, and a great help—and besides, I keep worrying she's going to see my car on the island and wonder what I'm doing here!"

Zarina gathered her purse and keys and walked past a wall where crops, whips, switches, handcuffs, blindfolds, ropes, spreader bars, and other BDSM tools were neatly arranged on hooks and shelves. A chain and black leather sling in the corner was a bit more hard-core than the typical suburban "sex swing" from a toy party that usually ended up as a plant holder. The film set was busy and she was sure to remain quiet as she passed the dominatrix and her submissive; the two women were readying themselves for the next scene. Girl-on-girl BDSM was hot on the website right now. As the site's statistician and web traffic analyst, Zarina made recommendations to Jo about what stories and film clips were getting the most hits. As the more creative director, Jo, who was a world-class dominatrix herself, seemed to have good instincts when it came to knowing what women wanted to see in both the straight and gay portions of the vixenden. club world.

Their site was meant to bridge a gap in the online world of sex. Needless to say, there were tons of porn available for those who wanted it. But for the more "vanilla" set, there wasn't much in the way of classier, more subtle arousal on the Internet. That's where Jo and Zarina's site came into play: curate some of the better sexy content from around the web, screen out the hardcore, tacky, or overly violent stuff, and produce original material that was just what couples needed to start off a hot night at home after the kids went to bed.

As she got into her car, Zarina smiled thinking about Jo's schoolteacher comment. Would the parents be surprised "Miss Jo" ran a sexy website? Sure. But they'd be even more shocked if they saw her in full pro-domme costume, starring in one of her own videos.

"THAT'S A wrap, ladies," said Kevin, the director of the video, and the actresses headed for the changing rooms. He walked up the steps to the studio and entered. The producer, Lorena, removed her headset, exchanged a few words with Kevin and their executive producer, Jo, and headed off to her job at the local radio station in nearby Easton.

"Were you happy with today's work?" asked Kevin. He absentmindedly ran a hand across his close-cropped silver-white hair. At fifty, he was retired from his job as a pilot for the Naval Academy, but the military haircut had remained for his unexpected second career in erotic film directing.

"How dare you announce that scene was a wrap without checking with me?" asked Jo, angrily pulling her jet-black medium-length hair into a ponytail. She narrowed her steely blue-gray eyes.

"I beg forgiveness, Empress Josephine," said Kevin, lowering his hazel-green eyes.

"You know what this means," said Jo, unbuttoning her white linen blouse to reveal a contrasting black leather bra. Kevin had already noticed it through the fabric, and his body was reflecting his arousal.

"The dungeon?" Kevin asked, his eyes still cast downward.

"Exactly," said Jo. She noticed his arousal, picking up the remote control from the equipment table and running it across the bulge in his pants. "And there will be extra punishment for this exhibit of your lack of self-control."

"Yes, ma'am," said Kevin, braving a glance directly into her eyes, a twinkle of mischief in his own.

"Meet me in the dungeon in five minutes—I need to clear this studio," ordered Jo.

Kevin nodded his agreement, his hands clasped in front of his arousal to shield it from her penetrating gaze.

Jo walked briskly around the studio, thanking actresses as they left the studio to head toward their cars and jobs in waitressing and house cleaning. She locked the doors. Vixen Den Enterprises wasn't the location of anyone's full-time job. Although the company was profitable, Jo didn't want to leave the safety of her full-time benefits package at the elementary school where she taught.

Right now the only package she was concerned with belonged to a madly sexy former military pilot she wanted to dominate. She walked over and slid a large hanging wooden door across its rusty, creaky track. She actually enjoyed the old industrial setting for the site of not only her side business, but the playing out of the very real fantasies that were part of her dominatrix lifestyle.

She walked down a set of wide, dark steps to the partially underground dungeon space, opening a huge metal door to enter. Once a refrigerated holding area for the fresh catch of the day, the space received its light through chipped-paint windows cut high into the metal walls. Glass block had been used in the construction of the openings, which offered privacy to the space while still allowing the natural light of the outdoors. Today the room was a gloomy gray, darkening as a storm gathered on the horizon of the Chesapeake Bay outside the walls.

She looked down at the music selection on her phone and

turned on "My Lovin'" by En Vogue.

Kevin had removed his clothing and stood against the wall between the windows, his head down, hands clasped in front, awaiting instruction. He had learned this routine over time and after extensive punishment sessions. The sex was consensual, outlined in a detailed contract created at the beginning of their passionate, ongoing dominant-submissive relationship.

"Kneel," said Jo, and Kevin did as he was told, regardless of how cold and hard the poured concrete floor felt on his knees. His loins throbbed in anticipation of her every move. He'd never been a part of a relationship like this; in fact, had discovered Jo through her own website, where she had been testing the "Bonds" personal relationship meet-up section. Members could view one another's profiles, video chat online, and set up meetings "IRL" (in real life) at this section of the site. Jo was perusing the Bonds page and accidentally discovered the new curious member Kevin, a traditional vanilla, who would be a virgin to the BDSM lifestyle. *I need someone to take charge of me*, he'd written. Jo noted his Maryland location only an hour from the island, raising an eyebrow at the photo of him in a dark military jumpsuit uniform on a plane. She was transfixed by the contrast of his mysterious green eyes, the sexiness of that early-gray hair, the confidence of his smile. She would take control of this new member with a direct, personal welcome. She removed his profile from the website, sent him a private message, and claimed him as her own. *I will take charge of you*, she'd written to him. Now, a few months later, his post-military film directing hobby that started out with wildlife had been transformed into coverage of the human species' wild lives instead.

Jo walked over to the huge iron hooks on the heavy steel walls that once held seafood packing equipment. Some of the original nautical rope remained, but only for show because of their harmony with the theme than for actual use — those ropes were too thick for practical use. She ran her finger across the silk ties and blindfolds that were neatly arranged over a clear fishing line between two old hooks. She selected a simple red silk blindfold; its ends featured a slightly grittier texture for easier tying behind the head. She placed it on a small table next to him.

("Maybe next time you'll give your woman a little respect...")

She glanced over at Kevin — his head was, as it should be, downcast toward the cracked, whitewashed concrete floor.

She took him by the wrist, and after he rose to his feet she walked him over to the large wooden X-shaped St. Andrew's Cross in the corner of the room. Thunder rumbled outside. Jo lit four massive pillar candles on tall iron stands in the corners of the room as it grew ever darker in the sky, stealing light from the room around them.

She walked across the space to a large, wooden cabinet, custom-built using old wooden floorboards. He twitched ever so slightly when he heard the creak of the cabinet door opening; he knew what it meant.

Several dozen whips, crops, cat-o-nine-tails, and other devices hung in a neat array. Jo ran a manicured finger over the selections, thinking. Facing the cabinet, she unbuttoned her blouse, dropping it gently onto the floor. She could feel the heat of his gaze; knew she could turn around and catch him in the act of watching her without permission. She let him watch as she removed her long black skirt to reveal the black leather garter belt and panties that matched her bra, the French stockings with their single black seam down the backs of her perfect, shapely legs.

Kevin took the risk of watching her, knowing if she turned and saw him, his ass would literally pay for it later. His dick pulsed with its own heartbeat, filled with longing for her — the sweet anticipation of his time in this sacred, energy-filled space with her. Lightning struck outside as he waited, waited…

She picked up a small cat-o-nine-tails with long, thin strips of leather bound at one end with a firm leather handle. She turned to face him, noting that his eyes were probably only recently turned downward. Suddenly, she cracked the worn leather against the wooden cabinet. He jolted slightly. She walked slowly across the room in her four-inch red patent leather heels, placing the whip on the table beside the blindfold, which she picked up.

"Lower your head," said Jo. "And kneel."He did.

"I see you still can't seem to control yourself," she added, glancing down at his arousal.

He raised his eyes to her to determine whether she

expected a response.

"You may answer," she said.

"I've tried, but when it comes to you, Empress, I have no control," said Kevin. The candlelight reflected in his sexy green eyes and Jo began to feel a familiar tingling between her legs. Her nipples grew hard in a room chilled by the impending storm, as thunder rolled again. This would be fun; she loved the anticipation of it.

"I see," she said, a smile playing at the corners of her mouth. "Well, it seems I need to remind you of your manners."

She walked behind him, securing the blindfold around his head. He took in a breath when she pulled it tighter to knot. "Stand," she directed. He stood.

The next song on her playlist began. K.Flay. She smiled.

Jo took the cat-o-nine-tails in her right hand and walked behind Kevin, admiring his strong shoulders and firm ass, slightly clenched as it was under the circumstances. She knew the sound of her heels on the concrete floor was what made his butt cheeks clench even more tightly. She raised her arm and brought down the whip, with a medium amount of pressure, on his left butt cheek. He flinched only the tiniest bit. She switched the small whip to her left hand and bent slightly to drag it slowly from his left ankle up to his left butt cheek, where she paused, slapping him with her hand, hard. She lazily grazed three fingers across the red mark she'd left on his ass with the whip, feeling his goose bumps rise. She traced the fingers across the middle of his back and around to his left front nipple, which she felt stiffen as her fingers took it in, twisting slightly and pinching hard. She gently caressed each of the areas she'd reddened.

("If you like S&M, go choke a bitch...")

Kevin could barely stand. The sensation from the spanking was so exhilarating, and the sudden softness of her skin such a contrast. The nipple pinch brought another wave of desire. He felt weak in the knees.

She seemed to sense the weakness. She walked around to face him, placing the leather loop on the handle end of the whip in his mouth so its leather tails dangled across his neck and chest. Taking him by the wrist, Jo reached up to shackle his hands one by one to the St. Andrew's Cross. The modern bondage device was primarily steel and leather, though it conjured images of older wooden cross styles. It was hinged and could invert to different angles as well as rotate to any degree. She bound his feet into the leather and metal shackles, tracing the whip's tendrils along his abdomen after removing it from his mouth.

"No way to hide yourself now," she said.

Kevin, now blindfolded, could only hear her to try to anticipate her next move, and with his hands and feet bound, he felt himself give in to her control. His years of military training, of piloting planes, even in wartime in the Middle East, meant he was used to being the one in the driver's seat. But it had been a lifelong fantasy of his to be dominated by a woman—and he had told her when he signed the contract that he couldn't be more pleased it was finally coming to life.

"You have been quite noncompliant today," said Jo. She gently grazed the leather tails across his right leg, then his left, tapping them with only the smallest amount of force on the side of his upper left thigh.

Kevin spoke only one word: "Forgiveness."

"Repentance," responded Jo.

She grazed the leather tails across the surface of his complete arousal, watching as his dick twitched in response to her, glistening at the tip. She took a single finger and rubbed the very end of it, only for the briefest touch. She heard him take in a breath.

"Mmm," she said, as he heard her lick her finger and smack her lips. "This reminds me that I'm hungry."

He exhaled slowly, waiting for her next thought, her next motion. The rain pelted against the glass block windows as the wind whistled, rattling the old wooden doors. His eyes had adjusted to the darkness behind the blindfold enough to see the flickering of the candlelight at the edges of his vision, masked though it was in a tight silk embrace.

Jo turned the heavy metal crank on the side of the large St. Andrew's device clockwise, and click by click, the angle of the cross changed. Kevin was rotated onto his back almost as if on a spit until she stopped the rotation and he was splayed almost completely flat, his head raised only barely, his arms and legs extended in their X-shape.

Kevin heard the tapping of Jo's heels as she opened a

cabinet door, closed it again, slid open a drawer, closed it, and returned to his side.

"You are my table," said Jo.

He felt her place something small and solid on his abdomen, holding it in place as, *holy shit,* she began to cut it with a knife, slowly. The smell of the apple filled his nostrils. He concentrated on not moving. She cut only part of the way through the slice, popping the rest of it off. He heard the metallic clank as the knife landed on the table beside him. He felt a tiny trickle of juice drip down his side as she placed the apple face down in the center of his belly.

And, *oh, God,* the sweet, unexpected sensation of her hot tongue as she lazily licked that drop of juice from his side. Sounds were louder when you couldn't see, and just as a sudden crash of thunder ended he heard the sharp crunch as she took a bite from the slice of apple she'd cut. She picked up the knife, cutting another slice from the fruit that rested on him. His abdominal muscles tensed despite his efforts to relax them.

"Trust," she said, putting down the knife again.

She slowly dragged the slice of apple along his chest as she licked another stray drop of the fruit's sticky liquid from his body. She traced his right nipple with the apple slice, watching how his lower half reacted. She placed the piece into his mouth; he hungrily accepted it. She cut another, using his body as the table. This time, she traced the slice down the lower half of his abdomen, gently across his thighs. She took it into her mouth, sucking a bit loudly. He listened to the sounds of this, growing ever harder. She returned the apple to his engorged dick, tracing it up and down, slowly, circling it around the tip, returning it to her mouth to suck again.

He ached for her. His ass muscles arched against the steel of the cross. His rippled chest muscles, shoulders, arms, legs — every muscle in his body stiffened along with his cock, ever harder, as he waited for her to quench the unending hunger he had felt for her since the initial moment he'd laid eyes on her, long before she had ever tied him up in this dungeon.

Jo allowed her tongue to trace this aching hunger, to taste him for one brief moment before simply placing the apple slice into her mouth and eating it, chewing slowly. She placed another piece of the apple into his mouth.

She quickly slapped the cords of the whip across his abdomen, leaving a pink mark. She placed the whip down on him gently, letting its weight leave her hands, its handle on his chest, taking four leather tails and winding them around his arousal.

"I have a lunch date with Eva," said Jo. "So I'll be back to see you when I am ready for my dessert." She gathered her clothes and left him as the storm beat on the windows and he smiled, ever waiting, tense with the knowledge of her power over him.

THE SEMI-RETIRED corporate attorney Eva Bradley shook the rain off her oversized cotton T-shirt and stretchy black yoga capris as she entered Paul's Café and looked around to see if her friend Jo was already there. The late spring storm had caught her off guard, as island storms always did; she never managed to have an umbrella ready. The one from her car always ended up on her porch.

Seeing Jo wasn't there, she used the time to sit and collect herself. Herman, the chef, was ever busy, now icing one of his delectable Smith Island cakes with its endless layers. She didn't bother saying hello so he wouldn't have to look up from his concentration. She wondered what cake flavors were available in the back case today. She'd had quite the sweet tooth in recent weeks since the nausea had passed, and a slice of the orange cream cake (or *mmmm*, maybe she'd stop by for some of Patty's salted caramel cheesecake from the country store on the way home, too), delicacies she hadn't really appreciated before on the island, she now craved at least a time or two a week.

Nathan had brought her a cream cheese Danish that morning already from Paul's, so she'd better slow down with the pastries if she didn't want to end up the size of a...

Jo breezed into the café, apologizing for being late.

"It's fine," said Eva, "I was just sitting here fantasizing about cake."

"About cake?!" said Jo. "That doesn't sound like you."

"Well, it usually isn't," said Jo.

Eva had kept the secret for months, but knew that in a very short time the world would know. Even though she'd had months to get used to the idea, she was still somewhat shocked herself that at the age of nearly forty-three and with sons graduating from high school (thank the heavens) next month, she was nonetheless going to be having a baby in early September. Definitely not in the life plan.

Jo cocked her head slightly and narrowed her eyes, trying not to obviously glance down at Eva's oversized shirt. *There is no way*, she thought. And yet, of course, the number one question you *never ever* ask a woman, even a woman who appeared to be fully nine months pregnant, is whether she was pregnant. But Eva smiled at her.

"Buttttt, you just suddenly like cake now?" said Jo, cheerfully grinning at her friend.

Eva laughed. "I freaking love cake now. And let's just say I might have a tough time bending over to go sea glass hunting for a while."

"Oh no," said Jo. "*No fucking way.* Just no. You can't be..."

"Sigh. Yes, I can be. I guess I didn't pay attention to that movie in fifth grade," said Eva. "Looks like just when I thought my nest was empty, there might be another little one showing up in it."

"I don't even know what to say!" said Jo. "We're happy?! Right? You're happy and we are happy about this news? I mean because obviously if you didn't want a baby, you wouldn't be having one or you'd be giving it up for adoption to some poor infertile couple or something…"

"This is why I love you," Eva said, laughing again. "Your honesty. Yes, since I'm in my forties I'm in full command of my reproductive decisions and rights. And yes, I'm surprisingly happy even though I will be a single mother for the first time."

"A single mother because…" Jo began.

"Let's just not even go there," said Eva, a shadow crossing her blue-gray eyes.

"Fair enough!" said Jo. "Let's just get some lunch. With cake for dessert!"

"Yes. Enough about me. What's new in life as a kindergarten teacher?" asked Eva. "Glad the school year is coming to an end?"

"Oh, just the usual," said Jo. "Bossing kids around. It's the off-season, so no kids, but I'm tied up with a halfway-done summer project, so have to get back to that soon. I actually have a secret of my own I was hoping to share with you."

"Great! Let's get that secret out on the table," said Eva.

WHEN JO returned to the makeshift dungeon at the former seafood warehouse on Matthew's Island, Kevin had drifted off to sleep. He awoke quickly and tried to pretend he had been awake the whole time she had been gone, but she could tell that he had napped. Both the knife and the cat-o-nine-tails had slipped to the floor.

"Bored, were we?" she said. The storm had passed, and

the room was bright. She walked around the room slowly, unbuttoning her blouse and tossing it onto a chair as she blew out the now-unnecessary candles. She picked up the whip and returned it to the cabinet, choosing a suede flogger from the wall. She gently ran its tails across Kevin's abdomen before placing it next to him.

TLC's "Baby, Baby, Baby" played through the sound system from the control room upstairs where she had turned it on.

"No, Empress, just saving my energy for your return," said Kevin.

Jo had brought a bottle of water with her. She stepped out of her black skirt and, now back in her sexy black leather gear, screwed off the top of the water bottle.

"We can't have you getting dehydrated," she said. She poured water into the cap and began dripping droplets of water onto Kevin's chest a drop a time. His nipple stiffened as a drop landed on it, sliding off his chest and onto the floor. She filled the cap again, tracing droplets up his neck and onto his chin. One drop touched his lips and he dared to reach his tongue out to lick it.

"Mmm, as your domina, I'll decide where that tongue goes next, slave," said Jo.

"Yes, Empress," said Kevin, struggling to keep the smile from his face.

She filled the cap again, letting a sip of water enter his mouth. She filled her own mouth with a capful and kissed him gently, taking his tongue into her mouth to suck on it for a brief moment. As she did, she brought down the flogger, hard, onto his thigh. He gasped audibly.

"That's for falling asleep while I was gone," she hissed.

The slap brought his body's full attention back to her. She slowly dragged the suede tails of the flogger across his erection. As research for her own BDSM videos, she'd seen countless crazy penis-bondage devices and was never really into that next-level kink. She and her viewers liked a subtle, classic bondage — dark shadows, some rope, sleek muscles, silky ties, but nothing massively painful or terrifying looking. There was already plenty of that out there. As a dominatrix, bringing a certain amount of pain to her submissive brought her pleasure. But she wasn't into the hard-core stuff. She'd leave that to the dominatrices who were, and did it well.

Kevin didn't even know the hidden camera was on now — she'd surprise him later that night while they were in bed watching a movie, but only if she thought it was something they could use.

"My lunch was fun," said Jo, "but I want my dessert now."

"Anything you want," said Kevin.

"I want everything on this table," said Jo. She pulled off the blindfold and lowered her head to kiss him.

"It's all yours," he responded, eyeing her black leather thong hungrily. As she trailed her fingernails across his chest, he wished he could return her touch. She removed her remaining clothing until she was naked — *so perfect*, thought

Kevin, *just gorgeous.*

("Cause if you're gonna get me off, you gotta love me deep…")

She walked over to a cabinet drawer, placing down the flogger and returning with a double-headed rippled purple vibrator, deftly applying lubricant to one end, turning it on, and teasing it across her nipples, pinching them into peaks.

"You're kind of tied up right now, and I'm horny as hell, so I'm going to get this party started," said Jo.

Kevin nodded his compliance.

She turned on the other side of the vibrator and mimicked giving it a hand job while he watched, his cock throbbing with jealousy. She smiled, lowering the vibrator to let it stimulate her for a few moments while her hand tweaked one of her nipples. Her head lolled back. He watched as she ground against the vibrator. He strained against the leather and metal restraints, longing to be the source of her arousal.

She stopped short of orgasming, walked over to Kevin, inserted one half of the vibrator into herself and let one half toy with his ass as she stroked him. She let this go on for a few moments until both of them were ready to explode, and then stopped, turning off the device and putting it aside.

Panting heavily, she turned to him, seeing the beads of sweat dripping down his neck, his chest—his own complete state of sexual hunger. She stood beside the St. Andrew's cross where he had been splayed flat for hours now. She pinched his nipples, hard. He gasped. She traced her tongue across his chest, slapping both his nipples so hard they became bright pink immediately. She stroked his rock-hard cock as she cranked the cross to the position she wanted, his head lower, swinging one leg over so she straddled the cross. She swerved her hips and lowered herself toward his tongue, taking him into her mouth; they pleasured each other orally until they were both ready to explode.

"Tell me your desire," said Jo.

"Whatever is your desire, Empress," said Kevin.

"*Bullshit*," said Jo. "Tell me your desire *now!*"

"*You*," he said. "Always you."

"Beg me to fuck you," said Jo. "*Beg.*"

"Empress, I beg of you," said Kevin. "I can't stand any more of this torture. I need to be inside of you. Please, take me inside you, *now*."

She made one more adjustment to the angle of the St Andrew's Cross—from experience, she knew exactly the position she wanted it. Facing away from him, she slowly squatted over his tight abs into a reverse-cowgirl position, taking his burning hot man candle of desire inside herself, Jo moaning with pleasure as she finally got where she wanted to be.

Grabbing the straps hanging from the ceiling above her for leverage, she raised and lowered her body to her preferred rhythm. He exhaled with pleasure, perfectly in sync with her movements. She used her strong abdominal and upper thigh muscles to move slowly in a rhythmic circular motion, up and down until both of them finally exploded in turn, Kevin loudly wailing with release.

The fingernail scratches on Kevin's thighs, red marks on his ass, and chafe marks on his wrists and ankles lasted for days. He texted Jo the next day, telling her that if he accidentally brushed against any of the sore areas, even with the water from the shower, it would make him hard with desire to return to the dungeon.

Chapter 2

Maggie's and Wes's Bento boxes arrived at their favorite lunch spot: a cozy Café Tokyo table overlooking Fritchie Creek in lovely historic downtown Keytown, Maryland.

"Wedding details please," said Wes, picking up his chopsticks and cutting right to the chase as always.

"Ah, gawd," said Maggie, brushing back a piece of her unruly auburn curls. "I'm gonna be fifty years old for chrissakes and it's my third wedding. Not exactly a blushing virgin bride, ya know?"

Wes laughed, covering his mouth and rolling his eyes. He adored her Boston accent as always.

"Doesn't matter," he responded. "Still a wedding. Also since you elected to have your boring straight wedding at Sharps Island Inn, the number one gay wedding destination in the entire continent, you can't let it be tragic. My friends Ron and Dale own the place and I won't let you."

He glared at her with eyebrows raised in mock horror.

Maggie laughed at her best friend.

"Feel free to gay up my wedding all you want. I really don't care. I'm not exactly getting a bunch of subscriptions to all the bridal magazines, you know what I mean? I just need to find a *not*-white dress that makes me look the least fat, and I want to have a memorable time with my family and friends and celebrate *finally* settling down in my life with the man I love."

"Again," added Wes. "You mean settling down with him *again*. Does it even count as a third wedding when you're marrying your first husband all over again?! Ew, this is turning into too much math."

"I don't do math," said Maggie. She sipped a spoonful of miso soup.

"Oh Christ, no, me either," said Wes. "Unless it comes to guest lists. Now who all's coming to this shindig?"

"Oh gosh, maybe fifty people, just friends and family," said Maggie. "I'm dreading all the flowers and the hullabaloo."

"Well, good," said Wes. "That means Paul's will be able to cater us some better food than if it is a smaller crowd. Crab *everything* and is it too gay for you to have a rainbow-striped Smith Island wedding cake? Those things are delicious *and* stunning."

"I think that sounds awesome," said Maggie. "Who wouldn't want a rainbow wedding cake? Even straight people like rainbows! Stop being so heterophobic."

"Well, miss bi-whoosie-whatsie, I'm not sure you're the

straightest road on the highway!" said Wes.

Maggie poked a chopstick playfully in his direction. "I prefer the winding, scenic roads," she said. "I have certainly found they're always more fun."

"Well, *duh*. So what *are* you going to wear?" asked Wes. "Something delightfully vintage and fierce from your shop, I imagine?"

"Notta clue," said Maggie. "Honestly, I just keep hoping something sorta just shows up one day. I've been browsing eBay, but I don't really know what I'm looking for in the first place, so that doesn't help. Plus you can't try on dresses from the Internet, especially when it comes to vintage. I'll find some old thing."

"You'll find something. We can do a day trip to Greenwich Village. Oh *jinkies*, I just thought of something," said Wes. "What about our adorable baker Lisa? Can we even *let* Paul's do the cake on the island? Wouldn't she want to do your cake?!"

"I thought about it, and I can ask her," said Maggie, "but I hate to make her lug a cake over the bay bridge from the Western Shore on Labor Day weekend, right? But then how can she *not* do the cake? Also Eva said she's going to have her do the bridal shower cake at our girls' weekend, and she's gonna do some favors for the wedding too, so she'll be busy."

"Oh, fab," said Wes. "Plus there's always the wedding cupcake solution. Herman at Paul's can do the rainbow Smith's Island fabulousness, and Lisa can do some gorgeous groom's cupcakes in a ring around the cake, something like that, whatever. You can never have too much cake, simple as that. How's her man-candy graphic designer?"

"They are so adorable," said Maggie. "I'm so glad she's happy with Ben after all she went through with her husband dying, creepy as that guy was."

"*Right?* A foot fetish. And then he falls down the steps. Irony. Gothic. *Shivvver,*" said Wes. "Like some kind of damn Alfred Hitchcock movie."

"Ugh, dead husband drama, the whole thing was awful. Well, speaking of husbands, how's yours?" asked Maggie.

"Alfie is alive, happy, and well!" said Wes. "The marriage therapy really helped us work on communication and just typical married bullshit. He's still been hesitating on the baby thing, so that's been the main conflict, but I've secretly been talking to a few adoption agencies and wow, what a massive hassle, and the international thing would take *forever*, but time will tell."

"You guys will be amazing parents," said Maggie. "I know it will work out, even if you just show up one day on the doorstep with a baby, like teenagers do with a kitten, and then the parents just have to keep it?"

"Oh my God," said Wes. "Ha, HA! I know that in my heart we will be good parents and decide together. I just wish he was more on board with the whole thing—he's still annoyingly dodgy when the subject comes up. A baby is more serious than a kitten, isn't it? Because I think I could probably get away with the whole kitten thing. 'Oh hey honey? How was your day? Yeah, mine was fine. Listen, I got home from the Whole Foods and look what was hanging around by the back porch! It looked hungry and so I fed it. I think it's a stray. Can we keep it? *Pleeeeeeassse?*'"

"If anyone can get away with the kitten routine, it's you," said Maggie. "Also, just a reminder that he loves you! And that he really does want a baby, he's just afraid of what it means. The 'oh my God my youthful wild days are over' thing."

"Yeah, well *boo freaking hoo*. I mean I get that he's younger, but *I'm* not getting any younger, so then I worry I'm just too damn old for the whole thing," said Wes.

"Well, you're barely over fifty, so suck it up, buttercup," said Maggie. "Parenting is fun. Not every day. Some of the days. You and Alfie will work it out. You'll be fantastic once that baby magically shows up on your doorstep one way or another. So once you get ahold of the little muffin, have you decided on a move out of the city?"

"We love the city. We work in the city. Alfie is getting acting work in DC and Baltimore, so if anything he'd love to move to a bigger city," said Wes. "Yes, I'd love to have a yard for our adorable future baby and puppies and real kittens, but I don't know if the *yards* are in our *cards*."

"Thank you, Dr. Seuss," said Maggie with a laugh. "You don't need a big yard to raise living creatures. Dave and I raised the girls here in Maryland's second largest city of Keytown and they turned out fine!"

"Yes! How are your all-grown-up girls?" asked Wes.

"Amazing. Lilith is finishing up her second year at Syracuse and Erica got an internship this summer up in Philly. It will be lovely to have them as my bridesmaids at the end of the summer!" said Maggie.

"How gorgeous is *that* waterfront sunset photo shoot going to be?" said Wes. "Those family photos! I can just see them now."

"Me too," said Maggie. "Mmkay, so can you keep a secret? It's kind of huge."

"No," said Wes. "Not for five damn seconds and you know it. Also why have we been here this long and you haven't told it. *Go.*"

"Jesus," said Maggie. "This is why I haven't told you yet. I'm not supposed to tell anyone!"

"Oh bitch, well you know you're telling me now, so *spill it*," said Wes. He bounced up and down slightly in his chair.

"Oh my God, will you stop," said Maggie. "You are like a damn high schooler."

"Bitch, don't insult me," said Wes, "I'm like a middle schooler. *Now tell.*"

"It's Eva," said Maggie. She sipped her water, looking slightly stressed. She really hated giving away the secret, but Wes was her best friend and she had to tell someone—even Dave didn't know yet.

"Oh God, don't tell me she's getting married too," said Wes. "To her pretty little French chef boyfriend in New York who she's been screwing for like forever?"

"Not that I'm aware of," said Maggie. "Though that might not be off the table if she finds out he's the…"

"He's the…???" Wes's eyes grew huge. "HE'S THE WHAT?"

"He's the father," said Maggie. "Of her baby. Since we were just talking about…"

"Oh my holy you *didn't fucking just even*," said Wes. He stood up. His napkin fell to the floor. He spun around in a circle. He sat back down. "You lie. You lie *like a motherfucking harvest gold shag rug*. We have been here for like practically an entire *Bento box* and you buried the lede and did not tell me that our very own bestie Eva who is totally on the wrong side of forty is *preggers*???? I thought she had a new adorbs fisherman island boyfriend?! Wait a *minute*. Does she know if Chef Charles is even the—? Oh, my… God."

In his excitement he'd actually broken out in a sweat, had now retrieved his napkin from the floor and was dabbing dramatically at his temples. He took a drink of water.

"Excuse me?" said Maggie, covering her mouth with her napkin to hide her amusement at Wes's dramatic reaction to the news. He was, after all, the theatre director in Keytown, so she would expect nothing less than these theatrics. "I'm glad you sat your ass back down before I slapped it down. Did you just say 'the wrong side of forty'?"

"Oh Christ, I just mean for that perfect body of hers and considering her boys are, um hello, *adult* aged!?" exclaimed

Wes. "And can we get back to who the damn baby daddy is?"

"We can't actually," said Maggie, "because it's not something we're really currently discussing at the moment."

"Did you ask? Did she mention?" Wes couldn't ask questions fast enough.

"I did not ask. She did not mention," said Maggie. "Next time I'm on the island if she wants to discuss it I am sure she will, but it's not something you just come out and ask your friend when she tells you she is unexpectedly expecting. She was obviously shocked by the news."

"Holy McDiaphragm fail, Batman," said Wes. "Did she forget how birth control worked? I can't believe the corporate attorney woke up one sunny morning and decided that now that her boys were flying the coop she would like to fill the nest back up and have a baby!?"

"I don't honestly know," said Maggie, laughing. "She's changed since her mother died and the divorce and moving to the island. And with the boys about to graduate from high school, she has a lot going on. It could just have been a genuine mistake. I'm not sure what's going through her head."

"Well, it's what went through her hoo-ha that's the game changer now!" said Wes. "Damn! Pull me up a chair and pop me some daggone kettle corn! I can't wait to see how this one goes. In other news, she should give *me* the damn baby."

"*Lordy.* I'm so glad your tackiness is part of your charm," said Maggie, shaking her head and sipping her green tea.

"Me too," said Wes. "Let's start a pool on due date and

whether she will have a boy or a girl."

"I just hope she and the baby are OK, especially if she is going to be on her own raising the child." Maggie cracked open a fortune cookie. "Only time will tell."

LISA SWAIN, owner of the Blackbirds Pie shop in Keytown, rolled lazily over and tapped the top of the alarm clock snooze button, buying another seven precious minutes in bed. Her messy blond hair spread across the satin pillow as she curled her naked body back into the warm, soft sheets and once again into the arms of her handsome lover, Ben.

He'd been propped up on one arm, staring down at her with a glint in his caramel eyes.

"Hey, you," he said by way of a morning greeting.

"No, not morning," she grumbled, burying her face under his fuzzy chest.

He laughed, getting out of bed.

"You're the one who chose 'baker' as a career, young lady," he said, heading toward the bathroom. "Is that what the paper said when you filled out that test in fifth grade?"

"Coffee," she mumbled, pulling the sheets over her head. Her caramel-colored cat, Brûlée, jumped up onto the bed, having been very patient, and nuzzled against her, reminding her that the bakery customers weren't the only ones who wanted her to get out of bed this morning.

"This is why we moved the coffeemaker to our bedroom

and set it on automatic, remember?" Ben laughed again, yelling from the shower. "So the smell of coffee would help you wake up on the early mornings when you had to get up so early to go to the bakery."

"Mhrphrmphhh," Lisa mumbled inaudibly from under the covers.

"Come on. Tell me again. What's her name? Mrs. Morgan or Mumphrey or something who comes in *evvvvery* single morning for her chocolate croissant at exactly seven-oh-five a.m.?" asked Ben. "Are you really going to let down that *poor little old lady* in her hat and coat? People depend on you in this town!"

Lisa checked her email quickly from under the sheets, looked at her calendar to see what bakery orders the day ahead held, and resigned herself to the fact that none of them could be filled from her current location under the sheets.

"Oh *fine*," said Lisa, tossing the comforter off her head and puffing air out from her lip to blow stray blond hairs off her face. She smiled at Ben as he walked in with a towel wrapped around his waist. "There you are, Mr. Morning Sunshine."

"That's better, gorgeous," he said, bending down to kiss her as his towel fell. She felt the warm steam come off his skin and she grabbed him quickly around his muscled ass cheeks, pulling him back toward the bed, toward her mouth.

"Hey! Meetings! Pies! Work!" Ben resisted, less so as she took him in. He glanced at the clock. The Superman alarm clock in Max's room wouldn't ring for another fifteen blissful minutes. They both might be a few minutes late for work this morning. At least they were already downtown; ahh, the benefits of commute-free living. He relaxed, enjoying Lisa's morning surprise.

Looking up, smiling, Lisa said, "Guess we better get our coffees now. We're running a little late."

"I'm not complaining," said Ben, and she stood up and placed her finger in that dimple in his cheek she adored so much. For the first time in her life, she was truly happy. She felt alive, sexy, fulfilled. Her miserable first marriage and its brutal end in the tragic but somehow not terribly sad death of her first husband was now behind her, and she felt like was a lucky girl to have a fresh start in life.

The day Ben had walked into her bakery from the graphic design firm to consult about the logo, she'd felt something stir within her. She hadn't been able to act on it then, desperate to remain faithful to her husband despite her desire to join the Scarlet Letter Society. At the time, she even lied about being an adulteress to be a part of their group. But now, finally, she had the love in her life that she'd always wanted; the thing that had always been missing. Someone who made her happy — the definition of which seemed to be a sense of contentment within herself, not always questioning whether she was supposed to be somewhere else, doing something else. That sense of inner peace she'd always been searching for was finally here: *the thing the movies were always going on about — this was really it.*

She pulled on her robe, walked over to the coffee machine, and prepared two hot cups of java as Ben got dressed.

She'd been very nervous about Ben's son, Max, and how he would respond to having a woman around. Ben's dysfunctional ex had thankfully moved away the year before and Ben had won primary custody so Max could stay in the local school where he was now in first grade. Lisa naturally hadn't wanted to do anything to upset Max, but having no children herself, she didn't know the first thing about interacting with a six-year-old. But time had passed, she'd gotten to really know him, and Max was a great kid. He was also a kid whose mom, who had some issues with prescription pill addiction, had announced one day that she was moving to Portland Oregon with another guy. She only saw him now on holidays and for a two-week summer visit with her parents required to be present. Max took the whole thing very bravely, lucky to have such an amazing dad.

Ben took his coffee, thanking Lisa, and walked down the steps of the three-level historic brick row house in downtown Keytown to the kitchen. The building was serendipitously situated a few blocks from the advertising agency where he worked as head of graphic design and a few blocks from Lisa's bakery. Even better, and what had been important when the judge made the custody decision, though a number of other factors had obviously been involved, was that Max's school was in the neighborhood as well.

Lisa got dressed, thinking about how she loved visiting

her friend Maggie's vintage clothing shop in town and of course they had coffee dates often at Zoomdweebies coffee shop, though they missed the third Scarlet Letter Society member Eva now that she was on Matthew's Island pretty much full time now. Lisa brushed her teeth. Funny how the years passed, she thought. Eva's sons were graduating from high school in June, so Lisa was going to be helping with the party and couldn't wait to make their cake. She knew Eva couldn't wait to watch them cross that stage. Lisa put on earrings, slipping on shoes and taking her coffee as she went downstairs.

"Hi, Max!" Ben grinned as he greeted his son, who was just finishing pulling an Orioles shirt over his head.

Max ran across the kitchen to give his dad a hug.

"Frosted Flakes or Pop-Tarts?" Ben asked.

"I don't have to eat anything healthy?" asked Max suspiciously.

"You can eat a banana while we walk to school," said Ben, chuckling. "We're running a few minutes behind today."

Max turned to Lisa, hugging her as she walked into the room. "Hi, Lisa!"

"Good morning, buddy." She smiled in return.

"It's career day at my class and I need someone to talk to the kids about their job," said Max.

"Do you want me to come back in and talk about graphic design again? I'd love to!" said Ben.

"No, Dad," said Max. "You did that last year already. Lisa,

do you want to talk about being a baker?" asked Max.

Lisa looked up from her granola bar and coffee. She looked at Ben. Her face reddened. She willed the blood to go back down her neck. It had only been two short months since she and her cat, Brûlée, had spent nearly all of their time at the brick townhouse downtown, and she and Ben had been so careful not to "make a big deal" out of the relationship, acting casual, not wanting Max to be threatened or upset by her presence. Lisa still kept some things at Maggie's apartment as though there was some sort of illusion that she didn't really "live there full time" for Max but was just "visiting." Clearly, this question was significant. Only parents were invited to career day. She was not a parent. How should she respond?

The silence had been a beat too long. Max, though, was too young for social nuance. Maybe a year or two later he'd have been old enough to notice her hesitation, find it awkward, say *forget it* and storm out, but not yet. Not as a first-grader. He rushed on.

"If you came to my career day, could you bring bakery treats for everyone?"

Lisa and Ben both laughed and finally Lisa just gave the natural answer.

"Max, if you want me to come to career day and talk about being a baker, I'd love to do that. And I could bring some chocolate-covered pretzels for everyone!" she said. "Maybe you could help me decorate them."

"*Hooray!*" said Max.

"I'm so happy about it too, Max," said Lisa.

"I don't want Mommy to come back anymore," said Max. "She doesn't live here anymore. Only Lisa lives here now. Lisa loves me more now. Do you, Lisa?"

Lisa swallowed the bite of her granola bar down with her coffee. She looked at Ben. Ben looked at her apologetically with a *kids say the darndest things* shrug of the shoulders.

"Now, Max, you know your mother loves you, she just lives far away," Ben said diplomatically. He had never wanted to say anything negative about her in front of Max and cause Max to feel resentment toward him later in life about it.

"Mommies live here every day," said Max. "All the other kids at school have mommies who live in their house *every* day. Lisa's kitty lives here *every* day and she comes here *every* day and she can just *be the mommy* now. *OK, Dad? OK, Lisa?*"

He looked up at her, his little face squished up, concentrating hard on these adult issues.

"Max, I love being here with you," said Lisa. "Your real mom will always be your real mom, but Brûlée and I can spend as much time here as you and your dad want us to because we love you and your dad! We aren't going anywhere, buddy. We're here."

"OK, Lisa," said Max, satisfied, cramming the last bite of Frosted Flakes into his mouth. "And I can be in charge of helping decorate the chocolate-covered pretzels when you come to my class."

Ben smiled at Lisa, who looked at him, eyes wide, making

the tiniest gesture of wiping her brow, but at the same time had an enormous grin on her face, and even though Max was going to be late for school, they sat together at the little kitchen island, eating with one another before they rushed around town, going about their busy days.

ONLY TWO miles from their kitchen island, at another kitchen island in a subdivision of cookie-cutter houses in Keytown at a neighborhood called Stony Mill, personal trainer (and former owner of the now-defunct Rocks "Private Fitness Club" that served as a secret swingers' club in the neighborhood until her house foreclosure) Kellie Muller sat on a barstool in her satin bathrobe drinking her coffee across from Keytown Police Chief Christopher Linden, who was in his uniform reading the morning paper on the stool next to her. She looked out the window and across the street at her old house, where two kids ran out of the house and piled into a minivan. She wondered what the finished basement looked like now. The landscaping rocks, once a symbol of the swingers' club membership and the parties that had gone on in those rooms, were gone, replaced by crepe myrtle trees.

She laughed when she heard a story in the neighborhood of someone moving into a house that still had the fake landscaping rocks at the end of the driveway. After a few too many drinks a swinging couple had wandered up the driveway and knocked on the door asking if a couple was

"DTF," only to be asked by the very confused new residents what "DTF" stood for. Turned out the new folks were not, in fact, *down to fuck* and when they found out they lived in a house with massive landscaping rocks standing like gateway-beacon-giant-balls inviting people to their doors, the objects were quickly removed.

Once the central location of Kellie's swinger membership club had been shut down (by her new boyfriend the chief of police) in what had become infamously known as the "*MASQUE-RAID*" thanks to the local news headline, the local swinger scene had generally become far more private and off the books. No more formalized parties, nothing on the Internet. Everything was private, word of mouth only, and much smaller. Swingers were still swingers in Stony Mill, that would never change; they just weren't so out and proud as they once were, yammering on about it for all the world to hear.

"So what's going on in the world?" Kellie asked absentmindedly, sipping her coffee and watching the soccer mom in her Lululemon yoga pants climbing into her car. Kellie's formerly red front door had been painted beige and now matched the rest of the neighborhood.

"You wouldn't believe it," said Christopher. "And I know I don't need to say you can't repeat it, especially at that gym of yours."

Kellie raised one eyebrow.

"Please," said Kellie, "like I'm going to take a chance of

screwing things up with the owner of my gym, the guy who literally saved my ass, kept me out of jail, helped me start a new life, and, um, whose roof I currently live under?"

"You don't need to give me the damsel in distress routine," said Chris, standing to return his coffee cup to the sink. He turned to face her. "You know as well as I do that you built that gym from nothing as a personal trainer. I was happy to help you get started. And I did keep you in jail for a few hours on that first night of your arrest after the station closed. But that was technically only because you asked me to."

He walked back to Kellie, spun her stool toward him, scooped her up by her toned waist into a standing position, and raised her chin to kiss her. She returned the kiss, tossing her long, straight brown hair out of the way.

"That was so fucking hot," said Kellie. "You really need to get me down to the station after hours and lock me up for something again."

"That can be arranged," said Chris, pulling her toward him.

"I'm going to think of something illegal to do," said Kellie. Her hands wandered.

"And I will be very pleased to arrest you for it," said Chris.

"I honestly don't know whether I was more turned on seeing you that night at my house in your Phantom of the Opera costume or the moment you walked into the interrogation room in your police chief costu—er, uniform," said Kellie.

"Yes, we generally call them uniforms, not costumes," laughed Chris. "Well, I had already fallen in love with you so long before that. His hands caressed the silk of her robe — so soft.

"Fucking stalker," said Kellie playfully.

"Just doing my job," said Chris.

"Yeah, staking out my house!" said Kellie. She grazed a finger across the front of his pants, only momentarily.

"The police department legitimately rented the house across the street from yours for investigation into the goings-on there because of the drug dealings of your ex, as you recall," said Chris. "Your little 'parties' were pretty much the least of our concerns, though you were on pretty thin ice with the law there too, Miss Swingtown."

"Didn't hear any complaints from you while you had me tied up with that leather whip, Chief," said Kellie, grabbing Chris's ass cheeks hard through his uniform.

"Aw, come on now, don't get me all hot and bothered before I have to go into the station and read boring reports and go to meetings all morning," said Chris.

"Why? Is there a serial murderer on the loose in this boring town?" asked Kellie, who had loosened the front of her cream-colored satin robe to reveal the erect peaks of her nipples evident through the nearly transparent fabric of her gauzy beige nightgown.

"Not that I'm aware of," said Chris, kissing her hard. "Just some online dominatrix porn ring investigation being run out of a local business, no big deal."

His thumbs went automatically to her aroused breasts. She moaned softly.

"Wait, are you kidding me? Well that sounds kinda hot actually," said Kellie, unzipping the fly of his uniform pants. "But you can't leave now. You haven't even had breakfast."

"Mmmm," said Chris, twisting at her nipples gently, then more firmly, as he knew she preferred. "I am pretty hungry now that you mention it."

Kellie unbuttoned the uniform shirt, taking care to remove and place it aside with her robe, as Chris took off his undershirt to reveal his abs, perfected at the gym they owned together, removed his pants and underwear, and placed them neatly over a chair beside the shirt. She ran her hands lightly, appreciatively over his chest, lowering her head to lick and kiss the rippled muscles there.

She walked over to the spinning carousel of matching black upscale kitchen gadgets on the gray granite counter. She turned away from him, and he walked over, letting her feel his extreme arousal against the thin fabric of her negligee. She arched her back, pressing her eager ass against him.

"What could I prepare for you for breakfast?" She spun the carousel, choosing a long, flat spatula.

"You are all I need, ever," he moaned quietly, weakened as always by her presence. She undid him. He would do anything for her.

She turned, slowly, taking him in one hand and rolling her

wrist back and forth, spreading her legs to place him closer to where she wanted him. With the other hand, suddenly, she slapped the back of his thigh, causing him to gasp out in shock. He laughed.

"Is this what's for breakfast?" he asked. He reached behind her to the gadget carousel and removed a thin metal whisk. Lowering one of the thin straps of her negligee and then the other until the garment slid down her body, he slowly dragged the cold piece of metal across her shoulders, bringing a shiver across her body.

"It's delicious," she said.

She transferred the spatula to the other hand and slapped him hard again, on the other butt cheek. He smiled, refusing to be deterred from his current course and also refusing to stray from his current gentle stroking style.

He grazed the spokes of the whisk across her shoulder blades in a zigzag pattern downward and just barely over her nipples. She sighed at the gentle pressure, wanting more. He ran the whisk down her abdomen.

She placed the spatula on the counter with her left hand, returning it to squeeze the red area on his ass cheek, and using two fingers on her right hand to continue arousing the tip of his erection, feeling him quiver against her. She heard the metal whisk land on the countertop and he brought a finger to her aching center, circling it at the perfect place; she pressed herself toward him hungrily, bringing both her hands to his stiff cock and bringing him closer.

Knowing they were both unable to wait another moment, he pulled away from her and lifted her in his strong arms once again over to the breakfast island counter, placing her atop the stack of newspapers. She looked at him quizzically, smiling. *The counter is too high…*

But in a moment Chris had grabbed one of the kitchen's perpetual items — the sturdy metal stepstool. Its first step was the perfect height for him to enter her. Chris had placed his left arm around her waist and she slid on those newspapers back and forth across the countertop like a kid's sled across the snow. With his right hand he used his fingers to expertly massage her clit as he lowered his head for a moment to lick, suck, and take in her nipple. She placed her arms around his strong neck; all she could really do was enjoy the ride. He raised his head again, pulling her hips toward him harder, faster.

Though she would've liked to, Kellie didn't last long with this overwhelming rush of sensations. She exploded into what felt like a full-body orgasm. Chris moaned hard as he released into her, his own bliss. Just as he did, they heard the explosion of Kellie's coffee cup hitting the tile floor. The stack of newspapers had slid it off the counter.

They laughed, disentangling themselves from the newspapers and remaining plates and stepstool.

"Well, that was the best breakfast ever!" said Chris. "Guess we need to get this mess cleaned up and maybe get something to actually eat." He leaned down to kiss her.

"It was one hundred percent perfect except for my poor Doug Sassi coffee cup!" said Kellie, returning the kiss, looking a bit sad as she put on her robe and picked up the pieces.

"Your what now?" asked Chris, smiling. He began getting dressed.

"The potter from Still Pond," said Kellie. "It's handmade!"

"Wow, I didn't realize your coffee cup is from the guy who made it. Is the guy still around? I'll buy you another one," said Chris, laughing. "It was worth it!"

"Agreed," said Kellie. "Yes, he's around! You have to drive up to Kent County to get one for me. He'd probably appreciate knowing it went out in style, but you can just tell him it fell in the granite sink or something..."

"Absolutely," said Chris. "I promise I won't forget. Now, what do you think about actual breakfast? Would you like to come into town with me and eat somewhere where they bring food to the table?"

Kellie laughed. "Well, I need to get a shower and get to the gym for class! But how about a lunch date instead?"

"Sounds fantastic," said Chris.

Kellie looked up from where she swept the broken pottery pieces into the dustpan.

"I love you," she said.

Chris stopped buttoning his uniform shirt. He reached down, taking the dustpan away from her and placing it in the sink. He put her slippers in front of her, worried she might step on a broken piece. She stepped into them.

Embracing her, he whispered into her long hair,
"I've loved you from the first time I stalked you."

Chapter 3

"I'm doing fine, Maggie," said Eva, sitting down on the worn wicker rocker as she held the smartphone to her ear. The view of the water always made her exhale. She knew it had to be good for the tiny life growing inside her.

"Of course I've been to the doctor... yes, I'm going to Annapolis... oh *right*, like there would be an OB/GYN on the island!? There isn't even a veterinarian! Or any doctor! I'm lucky to even be on the phone with you right now since they haven't even turned on the damn cell tower yet... Who knows?... Yeah, they built it but they never activated it... Yeah, that's phone companies for you. When are you coming down so we can go over this wedding stuff?... Oh great!... I'd love to have a girls' weekend.... Yes, see if Lisa can come!... We can work on the bridal shower... *a WHAT?*... No, I don't want to talk about a *baby* shower... Yes, I guess you can call it denial. I've decided to stay in a tiny bubble of denial for a few more weeks until 'maternity clothes' becomes an unavoidable part of my vocabulary. I will force myself to deal with everything then... Well, I'm just about to tell him..... Oh, well, um, no, he doesn't know either.... Because I don't know... *maternity clothes policy* and denial, remember?! *I have to wear maternity clothes to my sons' high school graduation, Jesus effing Christ.* Yeah, you and Lisa can help me deal with my lifepocalypse when you come down... OK... Love you, too, Maggie. Bye for now."

Eva gently rubbed her hand across her ever-slightly-bumped belly and pushed the "end" button on her iPhone 6 — she'd switched to the friendlier smartphone when she'd retired from her corporate America rat race in favor of the slower-paced lifestyle of consulting law and island life. She opened the tide app and checked the low tide schedule. She didn't know how long in the pregnancy she would be able to go sea glass hunting with Jo — or at least sea glass *bending*. She figured they'd still walk the island's few remaining beaches together and Jo would just get all the good pieces while she was along for the fresh bay breeze and exercise. She was actually thinking about getting one of those scoop picker-upper things because she couldn't stand the thought of not being able to sea glass hunt all summer long. Though they normally kayaked there, Eva couldn't do that as easily lately so she had been telling Nathan she had a sore back and asking him to use his small skiff to take them to a nearby beach with great sea glass on it — her favorite place.

Nathan.

No sooner had she thought his name than she heard the wheels of his truck crunch across the oyster shell driveway, immediately bringing a smile to her face. Dating a man of few words had certainly come in handy in a situation where she really didn't know which ones to use. She hadn't exactly browsed Pinterest for adorable ways to announce her pregnancy. She'd spent weeks considering abortion. As a divorced woman over forty with twin sons graduating from high school, it really seemed like the easiest, most reasonable option. Catholic upbringing aside, her parents were dead and she really couldn't think of a good reason to bring a child into the world.

And every time she went through that list of rational thoughts, *this happened.* Nathan opened the creaky wooden screen porch door and walked in. He took off his worn, fishing-gear logo baseball hat, revealing his mop of unruly salt-and-pepper hair. He took her in his arms and kissed her. She loved the feel of his prickly beard and mustache, the intensity of his dark steel blue eyes as he gazed intensely into her own mirrored dark blue ones from atop his four-inch height advantage.

"How was your day, beautiful girl?" he asked.

Always, always the first thing he did was ask about her day. One of many reasons why despite all more-than-many reasons she hadn't been able to stop herself from falling in love with the decade-younger waterman. There were a dozen great reasons why becoming a mother wasn't a convenient decision, and there was one reality, one truth: she was in love.

"It was just fine," said Eva. "I'm happy to see you. How was your day on the water?"

"Busy," said Nathan. "Still bringing in some oysters, crabs are starting to run."

"I have some more depositions scheduled for later in the week," said Eva. "The class action lawsuit against DNR is developing into a huge case. It's still hard to say how far we'll get with it, but it's definitely lighting a fire against the state and I think it has the potential to be a real three-ring shit show."

"It's David and Goliath," said Nathan, walking in to grab a beer from the fridge and returning to sit beside Eva on the porch.

"Well, then we hit them in the eye with the rock," said Eva. "This state needs to learn they can't bully watermen anymore with outdated, unrealistic regulatory expectations while at the same time expecting them to provide a billion dollars a year worth of seafood on the plates of Americans."

"Uh-oh, here you go, Judge Judy…" said Nathan, smiling.

"I'd love to have my day in court with these idiots," said Eva. "They sit in their cubicles in government buildings and issue stupid laws and regulations and have no idea what goes on in these watermen communities and how hardworking you guys are…"

"You're right," said Nathan. "I ran into the captain from the Delmarva fishermen's association up at the docks in St.

Mike's today and he was talking about how much work you've done. Anyway, I just wanted you to know how much we appreciate... how much I ..."

He paused and looked at her. "I am thankful..."

She swallowed a lump in her throat. The pro-bono work she was doing on behalf of the watermen community wasn't just because she was in love with her boyfriend. She honestly felt connected to this place because she grew up here, because of how her parents felt about this land, and because of the centuries-long injustice inflicted by the state on a hardworking way of life with a simple goal of feeding people.

"I know," said Eva. "You don't have to thank me."

She was proud to return to her community. The place she once wanted more than anything to get away from. She'd spent her whole life working to leave this place. She'd run so far and so hard — to college, to law school, to big cities and corporations and names on buildings in New York to escape the horrors of her childhood, her drunk father — but it all came back to this. You could take the girl from her home but you could never take the importance of her home and what the place meant from her heart.

"It's sunset," said Eva. "Take me for a boat ride, captain."

"Always," said Nathan. So they set out for Cattail Harbor and a sunset sail on the *Lady Grace*.

The wind and the water were calm as they sailed around the southernmost tip of Matthew's Island, where the Talbot River met the Chesapeake Bay. Eva liked to sail past the

Sharps Island lighthouse, the namesake for Sharps Island Inn, the spot at the southernmost point of Matthew's Island, where Maggie and Dave would be married on Labor Day weekend. The 1882 lighthouse had floated off its foundations and five miles down the bay in an ice storm (with the lightkeepers still inside) and was now partially tilted to one side, abandoned, endangered, and for sale. It was picturesque, and Eva and Nathan liked to fantasize about having a few million dollars, fixing it up, and living in it.

Nathan anchored the boat. Eva stood and walked over to the leather captain's seat, wrapping her hands around his neck in an embrace, admiring the sunset and the view of the lighthouse structure, leaning as it did at a dramatic angle, floating peacefully in the bay.

"I want to live in the lighthouse," said Eva.

"I know," said Nathan, turning to face her. He stood and kissed her. She returned the kiss eagerly. There was nothing sexier to her than Nathan in his "captain" mode: in full command of this majestic vintage boat. While she normally saw Nathan in his waterman's working boat, this vintage sailboat, one he'd worked to rescue and restore, this was his pride and joy — he'd spent countless hours polishing its hardwoods, scavenging boatyards and the Internet to find the rare, necessary replacement parts for repair. It was where he was happiest, and she felt that in his whole attitude when he was here.

Being pregnant, though it had made her feel awful in the

first few months, oddly seemed to make her want sex now. She'd learned from the doctor it was perfectly safe at this point. His kiss aroused her. It had been weeks since she had wanted sex. She felt her tender breasts swell as the Chesapeake Bay breeze blew between her and Nathan; her breath quickened. She darted her tongue into his mouth. He took her hair in his hands, brought her mouth closer. She wore an oversized T-shirt and capri leggings: standard gear lately. His hands went down her back, slipping inside her T-shirt and up the bare skin of her back. She shivered.

"That feels so good," said Eva. "Your touch."

"Plenty more where that came from," said Nathan.

He reached down, taking her T-shirt in his hands, and lifted it suddenly over her head. She laughed, looking around. They were far from land, no boats anywhere in sight, anchored in the middle of the bay. There was no one to see them.

Light as a feather, he gently ran his calloused waterman's hands down her arms, across her sides, across the tops of her breasts. Her nipples grew hard inside the silk of her pale aqua bra. She relaxed her shoulders, her head falling back, and he kissed her neck, running his tongue across her clavicle. She automatically brought her black yoga capris closer to his jeans, felt them grow tighter against her, the soft cotton of his worn T-shirt against her belly. In response, he put his hands around her waist, kissing her deeply, pulling her closer to feel his arousal. She leaned backward against the ship's wheel, which he grabbed in the nine and three positions to steady, pinning her there for a moment as she worked her hips against his stiff dick.

His hands occupied for the moment, she now used hers to explore the outline of his dick from the outside of his jeans. She traced it with her fingers as he moaned. She slipped her ring finger inside one pocket of his jeans, finding the tip of his cock, feeling the wetness that had formed there, gently rubbing, feeling the twitching motion as he responded to her touch. He loosened his grip on the captain's wheel, allowing her to take control of the ship. She unzipped his jeans with the other hand, inserting two fingers to rub the underside of his rock-hard arousal, reaching all the way in to gently massage his entire undercarriage area. It drove him wild. She watched as his eyes rolled back in his head, eventually closing, and he sighed with pleasure. He had dropped his hands from the wheel.

It excited her even more to see him in a state of full arousal like this. Her nipples rock hard, he looked down and seemed to enjoy seeing her this way as well. He rubbed her stiff nipple peaks, moving his hands around to her back to unlatch her bra and remove it. The bay breeze and the kneading motion of his rough fingers had her already-super-sensitive nipples aching for more. She gently rolled her grip across his penis with one hand inside his jeans, grazing her fingers across its wet tip through the pocket with the other as his whole body shuddered in response. The motion of the sailboat beneath them was gentle, rocking them as they moved against each other, barely able to contain their passion.

She dripped with wetness for him, feeling her clit now pulsing with anticipation for the moment she could match his own twitching need with hers. He lowered his hands from her breasts, reaching down to feel the wetness between her legs. He started to lower her capri pants, which she thankfully scrambled out of, letting them fall to the deck. He rubbed her clit expertly with two fingers from his right hand, keeping the fingers of his left hand in a gentle twist around her left nipple. She greeted the fingers of his right hand by pushing her hips forward toward him.

She gently lowered the waistband of his boxers and jeans, letting the items fall with the rest of their clothes to the deck. They were now ass-naked to the Chesapeake Bay and far too turned on to give a damn. She pulled him toward her to feel his hardness more closely against the softness of her ever-slight belly bump, using her fingers to rub the pre-cum between her tits.

Nathan was taller than Eva; she only had to lean down slightly to take his ramrod shaft between her swollen breasts. He squeezed his muscular ass cheeks, while Eva squeezed her tits together to form a valley for his shaft; he rocked against her for a moment while she licked and kissed his ripped abs, but wouldn't be able to stay there long. Watching a million diamonds of the dying sunlight reflect on the water, he let his eyes close, his salt-and-pepper-topped head falling back with pleasure in the fading daylight.

He stopped, bringing her face back up to his, leaning down to kiss her. She grabbed the back of his tousled hair, desperate, lowering her hands to pull his hips against hers. She brought her aching mons against him; she needed the pressure there, she wanted him so badly.

He placed his hands around her waist, scooping her up and lifting her, turning her around, and placing her down on the wide, soft, worn leather captain's chair atop its raised wooden platform. As he faced her, she immediately took him into her hands, bringing her lips to taste his saltiness, taking him in, but she would allow this only for a moment before stopping.

"Nathan, I need you," said Eva. "Take me."

The captain's chair had sturdy leather armrests, and she gripped them, opening her legs. If he stood on the deck of the sailboat below the platform on which the pilot seat rested, he was at the perfect height to reach her. He smiled. Lowering his head, he took her in with his mouth, teasing her clit with his tongue. Standing, he placed the tip of his cock just at the opening of her velvety wetness, using his fingers to arouse her further as she arched her back to try to bring him inward. The boat's motion was on her side as the Chesapeake Bay waves moved them closer to one another. He grazed the palms of his waterman's hands with the lightest amount of pressure over her aching nipples and she brought her hands down, one to grab the base of his cock, bringing it to its full hardness, feeling it twitch as she ground her hips in a circular motion, around and around against the amazing pressure, the other to gently graze her fingers against his tender, sensitive skin beneath while he rocked into her.

Nathan placed one hand on the armrest to steady himself as he made love to Eva and she grabbed his ass, screaming out in pleasure as she came, came hard against his motion in time with the waves of the bay. Nathan moaned out loudly too at the sound of her bliss, unleashing all of his desire into her in an explosive orgasm.

"Oh, God, Eva," he said. "So fucking amazing."

"Damn right about that," said Eva. She panted, trying to regain her breath and composure.

Nathan reached into a storage compartment for towels, handing one to her, gathering their clothes.

"I don't want you to be cold," he said.

"So sweet," said Eva, putting her things back on. "We have a few more minutes before we have to sail back? Let's sit and watch the lighthouse just for a bit."

Nathan dressed. "Of course." He embraced her, and they sat on the historic mahogany bench with the best view of the sun dropping toward the horizon.

"Would you raise our baby there with me?" said Eva, pointing toward the lighthouse. "If we won the lottery and fixed it up."

"Of course I'll raise her there with you," said Nathan.

Eva looked at him quizzically, smiling. "You know, don't you?" It wasn't a question. She had spent these months worried about how to tell him. How silly. He'd known all along; of course he had.

"Of course I know," said Nathan. "I see you every day. I just made love to you. I know your body! Your moods, your tiredness, your eating habits. I wasn't going to talk about it until you were ready."

"'Her?'" said Eva. "You said you'd raise 'her' in the lighthouse with me?"

"Oh," said Nathan, "well that's just an educated waterman's guess."

"Fifty/fifty," said Eva. "A waterman's guess is as good a guess as any."

She leaned toward him, resting her head on his shoulder to watch the gorgeous colors of a Chesapeake Bay sunset: the streaks of orange and yellow and red, and the cotton candy pink and purple clouds in the sky around it. And in that moment, watching the leaning lighthouse at sunset, it was decided. This baby was part of a new family.

Eva touched her belly again, what had been her secret for so long. So few people even knew she was pregnant. Her ex-husband and two sons had found out only the weekend before when she'd asked to have a "family" dinner. She couldn't wait any longer. Of course seventeen-year-old boys didn't look at their mother in a way that would recognize a first trimester pregnancy, but in another month even they would've known the truth. And since Eva's ex-husband was a pediatrician, the time had simply come. How humiliating was it going to be to attend her sons' high school graduation in a maternity dress? Oy, she'd think about that much later.

The dinner had been fantastically awkward. Joe had turned bright red. *You're what?* And the worst part had been the look on his face when she knew he'd been calculating whether there was any mathematical way the baby could have been his. There was most definitely not. And then to pile on the awkwardness, her son Calvin's innocent excitement. *Hey, we're going to have a little brother or sister – that's cool!* And his more cynical brother Graham's response, *You mean* half *brother or sister.*

Half, thought Eva, as her hand rested on her abdomen. Nathan of course would never wonder for a moment about the paternity of the baby. Why should he? He didn't know anything about her "goodbye sex" in New York with her ex-lover the chef, Charles, whom she hadn't even seen since. He seemed to be so far away, light years away from a past she'd left, her corporate life, its madness and money and stress traded for the peace and pace of this tiny island and a very different second half of her life.

She'd been to the obstetrician, who had explained the risks of amniocentesis, which Eva had remembered from what seemed like ages ago with the twins: miscarriage. She certainly wouldn't risk that in order to discover the paternity of the baby and besides—she didn't exactly have a willing participant for a blood test.

She looked over at Nathan and he smiled at her, beaming

with pride, so handsome in the ending light of day.

"I have something for you," said Nathan, returning from a small storage cabin near the cockpit to where Eva sat. "It's just a small gift. I've been keeping it here in the boat, saving it for something special, your birthday maybe... but I think today might be a good day, with this pretty sunset."

"What is it?" asked Eva, accepting the small box, pleased at the surprise.

"I just want you to know this isn't any kind of pressure or commitment, I don't want you to feel like it's too much or anything," said Nathan, "it's just something I thought you'd like so I had it made for you, just something to remind you of how much I appreciate you and...I love you."

Eva looked at Nathan questioningly; it was so unusual for him to do something so elaborate, to give speeches like this. She opened the box and gasped.

"Oh my God, Nathan," said Eva, holding her hand over her chest. She took in another deep breath. "This is just amazing, and it's the most thoughtful thing I've ever had anyone do for me."

"Try it on," said Nathan. "I brought the piece along with another one of your rings to Carter's Jewelry one day up in Easton so she could size it, I hope it fits OK..."

"My favorite piece of red sea glass..." Eva said. "It's perfectly stunning."

Nathan had taken Eva's most special beach find, a perfectly wave-tumbled, worn piece with raised round bumps (probably once an old piece of depression-era glass) shaped almost like a triangle, and had it set into a sterling silver setting, with a small diamond on either side. It made for a breathtaking piece of jewelry.

"I don't even know what to say," said Eva. "It's the most beautiful thing anyone's ever given me."

"I'm so happy you like it," said Nathan. "I know sea glass hunting is your favorite thing, so I thought you might like to wear your best piece, especially when there are rainy days you can't get to the beach."

Eva felt a wave of emotion at the thoughtfulness of the gesture, at his love for her. The red from the ring reflected the red of the fiery sunset. She put her arms around him and kissed him, so thankful for the love she had found on this tiny island.

"I love you, Nathan," said Eva, "and I will wear this ring as a symbol of our love. Thank you for this gift. I will cherish it forever."

"Eva, I will cherish you forever," said Nathan. They embraced, watching the sun dip just below the horizon line on the Chesapeake Bay beside the leaning lighthouse, perfect in its imperfection.

Nathan sailed the *Lady Grace* back to Cattail Harbor and the pair went back to Eva's cottage together. Nathan made sweet, gentle love to her. Eva thought about how there had been a gentle quality to their lovemaking in recent months. Now she knew why. She loved the fact that he had let her bring up the pregnancy in her own time. As he fell asleep beside her, she turned the stunning ring on her finger, its small diamonds glistening in the moonlight, and she couldn't help but wonder once again about the baby's paternity.

It wasn't like she was going to ask Nathan for a blood sample, though she had actually considered lying to him and saying that because of her "advanced age" the doctor wanted to run some diagnostic tests to determine whether their combined blood types triggered any warning signs for birth defects. She'd thought about it, but she couldn't do it. She refused to do an amniocentesis and risk miscarriage, also because of her age.

This Maury Povich/Jerry Springer "who's your daddy" situation would have to play out on its own, she thought bitterly, as Eva rolled onto her side, away from Nathan, feeling an inner sense of shame. She wanted so badly for him to be the father.

She thought of her one golden ticket, a solution. She'd done an Internet search on paternity DNA testing and been absolutely shocked to discover how very simple it was in this day and age to find out the identity of the father of your baby. You didn't need a blood test or an OB/GYN or a hospital. All you needed was $100 and an Amazon order and in two days with free Prime shipping, you were the proud owner of a "Quickee Paternity At-Home DNA Test Kit." *How trashy is that?* Eva thought.

Sitting inside the zipped lining of a suitcase in the guest

room closet of an upstairs bedroom was the test. All Eva had to do was find the courage to explain the situation to Charles in New York, ask him to do a cheek swab with a Q-tip and send it back in the mail along with her own swab, and when the time came, within three to five business days she'd know via email who was the father of her baby.

Chapter 4

Jerry Tilghman sat in his perch, watching the boats drift to and fro, east and west through the narrows past his small control tower. He had been a bridge tender at the Choptank Narrows Bridge for nearly twenty-five years. He'd raised the drawbridge between Matthew's Island and the mainland thousands of times; it was the nation's busiest remaining bridge of its type. A retired meteorologist for a Baltimore television news station, he had settled on the island with his wife, Helen, more than twenty-six years before, and quickly decided when he arrived on the island that the retired lifestyle wasn't for him.

The part-time position tending the bridge suited him perfectly. Three twelve-hour shifts a week had seemed more like a full-time job to his wife, and certainly made for some long days, but they didn't warrant full-time benefits from the Maryland Transportation Authority. In the beginning of his time as bridge tender, Helen had put up a bit of a fuss, nagging him her fair share about being away from the house. The truth of the matter was, they didn't have the money to travel the way she'd hoped, and they both knew the money from his bridge job was something they needed. She nagged him when he was there, nagged him when he wasn't, so he figured it evened out. But that had been back when she was alive. Eventually the cancer had stopped her nagging. He missed it.

"What other job in the world has a view of the sunrise and the sunset from the same spot?" he'd say to her, a smile on his face, but she'd knitted away, shaking her head. He didn't even think she heard him most of the time, but he knew at least she was pleased he wasn't in a job that was physically or mentally taxing. At the bridge tender's house, there was satellite TV, not that he ever watched except for an occasional news report. He had his crossword puzzles and his newspapers, and besides, with all the boat traffic, he was usually too busy to do any of that. The watermen came and went all day long, hauling crabs and oysters and rockfish to and from the various harbors, making their living. He enjoyed watching them, waving as they went by; they all knew him, at least most of them who cared to bother.

If he wasn't watching the boats, he was watching the weather. This year was shaping up to be the windiest, most erratic and stormy in some time. Jerry worked alone, but anyone who knew him could tell you that if Jerry got the chance, he'd talk your ear off about the rising water level or the increase in the rates of unpredictable, violent storms. But nobody wanted to hear it. Most of the watermen thought talk of "global warming" was malarkey. Jerry specifically never used words like that anymore for that reason. "Climate change" was a little bit better, he learned, but still sounded like a government conspiracy to many of the locals. So Jerry had adapted, tried to be more vague, and now only really talked about this "right crazy weather we're havin'" just to fit in.

Helen hadn't wanted to hear any of it anymore, either. She would knit and nod her head and manage a polite "of course, dear" as Jerry went on about how he'd been sitting there for a quarter of a century just watching the dramatic weather changes happen. He had a small can of black paint and a small paintbrush that he kept in the storage closet at the bridge tender's house, known as a tenderhouse to Helen and Jerry and other bridge tender families (though most people didn't know it was called that) and he'd dutifully marked the high tide marks of the storms on the underside of the drawbridge over the years. The high tide marks from Hurricane Irene in '03 and Isabel in '11 and even that most unusual "Great Derecho of 2012" that blew out the entire glass wall of the Matthew's Island Inn just a few years back—those black marks were all on the wall, with a lot of lesser-known high tide marks in between from storms that came and went when the Talbot River met the Chesapeake Bay in just the right wind conditions and the water rose and rose and sometimes

Jerry felt like nobody even noticed it happening but him. With Helen gone, *damn* cancer (she'd just been glad she didn't have any children who had to suffer through getting this awful thing, she had said) he didn't have anyone to tell it to, so he'd mostly just talk to himself, keeping notes in the bridge tender's log about the tide line marks. He kept a spreadsheet in Microsoft Excel — the charts and graphs showed the rising waters over a twenty-five-year time period. He reported all of his detailed findings to NOAA, though he wasn't ever sure anyone there really gave a rat's ass. He figured all the data he was keeping should go to someone.

As a former meteorologist, Jerry liked predicting the weather, and he didn't trust the existing computer forecast models out there that were basically a crapshoot. He'd devised a system of combining all the individual components from a variety of data- satellite, low pressure, wind speed, barometric pressure, cold and warm fronts, and other calculations gathered from reports he had access to from the Internet, thanks to a few friends back at the TV station and a few creative online underground methods he had learned over the years as well. He did a daily weather analysis and was able to compute a weather prediction model for the island on a daily and weekly basis that was more accurate than anything that ever came out of the major cities. A few of the watermen knew that Jerry could more accurately predict the weather than any other source — they figured it was just because he sat up his bridge tender's house and watched it all day — and had taken to asking him about it when they'd see him around town. It helped their boating business to know what to expect in terms of weather when they were about to go out on the water for the day.

The winds the night of that crazy derecho (the Spanish word for a damaging windstorm hadn't even been introduced into islanders' vocabulary until that storm) back in '12 had been off the charts for something that wasn't a hurricane. The tiny bridge tender's house had whistled and shaken until Jerry was sure it would fall apart. The state of Maryland had officially told him to evacuate, but Jerry stayed at his post, concerned that if a boat came through, it would need to be able to cross the narrows. He wouldn't want a captain to be stuck out there in those awful conditions. These were not pleasure boaters out in this weather — these were working boats. There weren't too many workboats big enough to even need the bridge raised, and he usually knew exactly which ones were out and which had already come back in, but that night there had been one boat he couldn't reach by radio. It was a boat that sometimes stayed out overnight. It was very possible the boat simply wasn't coming back in. It wasn't his job to babysit the boats, and no one expected it. And of course the boat could have docked up somewhere on the other side if it came back in and he wasn't there. But he just couldn't walk away from the bridge and leave the poor guy unable to get to his regular harbor on a stormy night like that.

So he waited. Tending the bridge. That was his job, wasn't

it? He'd actually told the state he had already evacuated his post. Didn't need to get their feathers all ruffled. Sometimes, he'd even spend the night at the bridge tender's house, unbeknownst to anyone. If his shift ended late at night and started early the next morning, there wasn't even a reason to go home, now, with Helen gone. The sofa was plenty comfortable. He'd shower and shave that next night. There were plenty of snacks and drinks in the small fridge, or across the street at the bait and tackle store, where he'd walk twice a day to exercise his legs and get a taste of the local scene. Having come in with their hauls for the day, the boat captains sat around, gossiping and drinking.

Jerry glanced both ways, seeing no boats coming and glanced at the clock; he found a rare opportunity for one of his twice-daily fifteen-minute breaks.

"Here comes Jerry!" one of the watermen called as Jerry walked across the street during the quick pause in boat traffic to get a snack. "Hey, who's running the bridge?" the crab boat captain joked. "I think I see a giant sailboat coming this way!"

"Well, they'll just have to wait while I get my Little Debbie snack and a Gatorade!" Jerry replied, lumbering up to the counter with his *Baltimore Sun* newspaper. "Sure isn't the end of the world, now, is it?"

The locals made fun of Jerry's preoccupation with what they considered the myth of "global warming." They knew about his measurements of the rising water levels, because they could see the black marks from their boats when they went under the drawbridge. All in good fun, they teased him.

"You come out from yer castle to measure that rising water ag'in, Jer'?" another boater asked, snickering, plunking a forty-ounce beer, a candy bar, and a bag of chips onto the counter.

"You wanna wait twenty minutes for that drawbridge to go up next time you come into the harbor with a boat full of oysters?" Jerry would answer in return, a half-mocking grin on his face.

Jerry didn't mind most of the watermen; in fact, he had a great deal of respect for almost all of them. The majority of them were hard workers who took care of their families. But there were a small percentage of the locals who proudly flew Confederate flags on their boats, drank far too much, used drugs regularly, and treated the women in their lives very, very poorly. They drove their boats drunk around the narrows, endangering other boats and especially endangering casual recreational boaters and innocent kayakers in the water. These types of "captains" he could do without.

Jerry returned to the bridge tender's house, happy as always to lock the door behind him and get back to work. As he locked the door, he thought of the time the police had come to the door and taken over the control of the building, when a drug bust was taking place. Jerry had been ordered to raise the bridge so that the suspect couldn't leave the island. Of course he'd done as he'd been told. The suspect had eventually been arrested. Apparently he wasn't much of a local—one of those guys would've simply hopped into the nearest boat to escape the island.

He knew there was a way of life that was dying off on the island, and it was sad. He missed one of his favorite fishing boat captains, the legendary, larger-than-life Harry Budson, who loved to tell tales of "raising the bridge" on someone who owed him money, to keep them on the island until they paid their debt, or notifying the bridge tender to raise the bridge on someone he wanted to keep off the island, like a state regulatory agency. Tales of women dying who had been born on the island and never once left it and other generational stories were ones he found quaint. He loved watching local kids come up to flatten a penny by placing it in exactly the right spot where the drawbridge, when raised, would return it to them, thin as paper. He appreciated and respected the history of the island.

Although the rough-around-the-edges locals could get a little raunchy, it was the wealthy weekenders who could really get on Jerry's nerves. Calling the bridge tender's phone line or radioing in to request the bridge be raised — these were often $250,000 boats that also managed to get stuck in the mud at low tide coming into the channel because they somehow couldn't manage to have a $250 piece of equipment or app on their smartphone to tell them the water depth or the time of low tide. He saw it almost every day in the summer. These pleasure boaters came in on these fancy sailboats and just had to sit in the mud for three hours waiting for the tide to come in. *Forget calling me to raise the drawbridge, jackass, you can't get through the narrows if your four-thousand-pound boat just tried to get through two feet of water.*

And these were the guys who didn't believe in rising water level, because they thought low tides meant the high tides weren't higher. They didn't seem to remember the fact that the island used to have beaches and now there weren't any, for the love of God, not to mention the fact that entire islands that used to be around them were now gone, completely underwater. Jerry talked to a guy one time who told him "the water ain't rising, the island is sinking." The sad fact of the matter was that both of those things were positively goddamned true.

Jerry pushed the large green button to raise the bridge for another seafood boater. He glanced at his computer screen, showing an early model for the upcoming hurricane season. This year was expected to be the worst storm season on record, and he worried about how the island would fare. He punched in a few keystrokes and looked at another model, again finding no differences. All his early calculations looked the same. He knew all it would take was one hurricane coming up the Chesapeake Bay the wrong way. The waters were calm now, but his numbers told him they weren't going to stay that way, and Jerry's numbers hadn't lied to him in the past. He watched the boat as it sailed from the majestic bay on the east to the stately Talbot River on the west, and he thought, as he had so many times in the past, God help Matthew's Island if those two massive bodies of water, separated by an island only a mile wide, ever got together. This island was what he had left to care about, so care he did.

Chapter 5

Jo paced the creaking wooden floorboards of the old seafood warehouse at VXD Enterprises. Zarina sat beside her in the glass office. No filming was currently going on below them on the production set floor; the space was empty. This meeting was just between the founders.

"Our page hits are doing really well," said Zarina, "the website traffic is growing month by month, and memberships are up."

"We have to give women what they want," said Jo, "but it can be tricky to figure that out. I think doing that survey of our current members is a good idea."

"Well, we know what they *don't* want, which is more low-budget, tacky porn aimed at men," said Zarina, "there's plenty of that already. Taking a look at the numbers, here's what we have: besides the obvious top hits on our dominatrix video series, our members like the erotic short stories. They like the erotica fanfic reviews, and the 'best of indie feminist porn' series."

"They seem to be coming to us to curate the web for them in terms of what is hot for women," said Jo. "Ninety-five percent of what's out there is disgusting for women to look at. It's derogatory, a turn-off, and basically jack-off material for guys."

"Mostly guys with crappy taste," said Zarina. "I actually feel bad for guys with good taste in porn. They have to look pretty hard, pardon the pun, to find the really high-quality material. Production quality is horrendous. The music alone. Agh."

"Being able to produce enough new original material is a challenge as usual," said Jo, "and it's expensive as shit. We're paying Kevin to shoot, and then we have the production staff, and of course these actresses and actors, who think it's fucking Broadway around here."

"*Right?*" said Zarina, with a soft snorting sound. "They're getting paid, and it's not some disgusting low-budget porn, so there are worse gigs, that's for sure. But this is an island on the Eastern Shore of Maryland, so I'm not sure why they think they'd be getting top dollar like they're in L.A. or New York. Seriously, guys, if you can go there and make that kind of money, by all means, be our guest."

"Also, we're offering them the opportunity to establish themselves with an online presence and following that they can make real money off of in time," said Jo. "They can go off and start their little 'Montana's Hooters Dot Com' crap sites later when someone gives a shit."

"Yeah, right now they just want to watch her slap a dude around and they don't care who she is," laughed Zarina.

Jo smiled. "As you are well aware, we would never refer to the dominant-submissive relationship in the community as 'slapping a dude around.' *Very* disrespectful."

Zarina rolled her eyes. "Joking, of course. Besides, as a married woman who owns a coffee shop in a small town, you know I'm just a business partner who runs the website and not a very active member in the 'community.'"

"I know," said Jo. "It's actually better for us. You give us the 'vanilla outsiders' perspective. Though I wouldn't mind seeing you around our side of the community once in a while to get some perspective."

Jo raised one perfectly mascara-applied eyelash at Zarina.

"Happy to be of service, O Dominatrix-in-Chief," said Zarina, giving a fake salute, but noticing the sexy glance. "Vanillaheads unite. But you know I haven't always been a hundred percent straight girl."

"Really?" said Jo, eyebrows raised. "Not sure you've told me that story. I'd *love* to hear it. You did mention something about your mom not being the straightest arrow, back when I met her that one time. In fact, I wish we could get your hot mom the college professor down here to act in a scene or two," said Jo, motioning toward the filming room floor.

"Oh, God no. Are you kidding me?" said Zarina. "My mom wouldn't come near this place. She isn't into any of this kinky shit! She was just here that one time with me to check out the island and you know I had to lie about what we do here. Besides, she's actually taking a sabbatical from the college."

"Oh?" asked Jo. "Where to?"

"Said she needed to get away from the small-town drama crap," said Zarina with a laugh. "She took off to the Caribbean for a semester to work on a novel. I can't blame her. Last affair she had in this town was with this nutty accountant slash blogger girl named Rachel up in Keytown who ended up in jail briefly for illegal prescription drugs and then ultimately landed herself in rehab right here on the island."

"Oh, you mean 'The Keytown Mouse' who was all over the local papers?" asked Jo. "Everyone knew who she was. Her sister lives on the island too. It was a big deal when she went to rehab here, like we were getting a Kardashian or something. One of the sound engineers was just talking about how she just got out of rehab and is hanging around here on the island at her sister's house. The sister's boyfriend is apparently a lowlife though. Ah yes, *Rachel* is her name, the one who broke up the big swinger sex ring in your smutty town!"

"Wonder why she didn't go back to Keytown when she got out of rehab. Yeah, our town is never boring," said Zarina, "let me assure you. The very famous Scarlet Letter Society who Rachel was so set on destroying for some reason used to meet in my humble little coffee shop. The one my husband is currently gracious enough to be operating so I can be here with your lovely self running this erotica empire."

"Well, then I don't think I'd be giving away any national secrets to divulge that one of my best friends, Eva, is a founding member of that secret scarlet society," said Jo with a wink. "I've never mentioned it before to you because it's such an exclusive group."

Zarina smiled. "I love those ladies, all three. I really got to know them during the many early morning meetings they spent at my place. Even opened the shop early for them."

"I've never had a chance to meet Maggie or Lisa," said Jo, "but Eva talks about them all the time and I am sure I would enjoy getting a chance to meet them one day."

"They're both great," said Zarina. "And I'm sure you will have the opportunity, since Maggie's getting married right here on the island over Labor Day weekend."

"Oh, of course, I should've remembered that from Eva— she's so excited," said Jo. "I'm sure the wedding will be lovely at Sharps Island Inn. Everything there is perfect."

"I've never been out there but I've heard wonderful things," said Zarina. "I know Maggie is really happy."

"Well, our own Kevin had a blast over there one weekend filming one of Dale and Ron's wilder big gay weddings," said Jo. "He had to hire two extra videographers. When the whole video with the music and everything was done it was quite the production and ended up with half a million views on YouTube. Listen to this: they filled the pool with *rainbow Jell-O and whipped cream*, complete with a layer of rainbow sprinkles on top."

"A half million views? Holy crap! How did they even?" began Zarina, laughing. "I want to jump into that pool filled with rainbow whipped cream!"

"Who doesn't?" said Jo. "I'd be in that pool party. That had to be a challenge figuring out how to make it happen, but it was so well edited with the music and everything by the end — I'm sure it made for a great keepsake wedding video for the happy grooms and their guests. And, you know, the Internet."

"Well, we managed to get way off topic," said Zarina. "Rainbow whipped cream will do that to a business meeting."

"Derails it every time," said Jo. "OK, what I was going to suggest is that we take a look at that SEO consulting proposal we got so we can optimize social media to match the keywords that are performing best. And I'd like to take a look at partnering with a few select websites that are running extremely high-quality video. If we streamed some really high-quality fetish stuff in our sidebar it would increase the amount of our content without increasing our production costs."

"So basically it would be advertising for the other sites?" asked Zarina. "What's the revenue model for that?"

"We need to think about the possibilities," answered Jo. "Could we do an exchange with the other sites or should we simply charge them for the space on our page? It's going to depend on traffic. Maybe we could run a "Kinkiest Video of the Day" feature in the upper right corner but charge it as a premium ad spot? Or run it as an affiliate ad?"

"I was thinking we could bring in that web ad consulting company from Keytown to make recommendations on profitability now that we are at a point where the site has really taken off traffic-wise and we are starting to see a big return on investment," suggested Zarina. "Let them give us some ideas on how to manage content from an advertising perspective, handle SEO, and optimize profitability. Start making some real money on this thing."

As the women spoke, a scene was being set below them on the filming room floor. Sound technicians were setting up microphones. A huge, four-post steel cage bondage bed was being assembled. Kevin had arrived to supervise the production. Two actresses, bedecked in matching leather bustiers, booty shorts, spiked gladiator heels, and a mixed variety of tattoos waited on nearby stools, water bottles in hand. Four men in bathrobes arrived intermittently. It was to be a complicated production, with a large camera dolly perched above the set to circle the scene and capture the action. Leather straps and metal chain links were suspended from the top rails of the bed that could be adjusted and tightened by the actresses.

The men were preparing to be handcuffed to the four posts of the bed wherein the dominatrices would do what they simply did best: dominate them. A metal cart not unlike a wardrobe rack was rolled into place offering an array of harnesses, belts, suede and leather floggers, spanking paddles, nipple clamps, bondage hoods and blindfolds, and other miscellaneous tools of the BDSM trade used in filmmaking.

Kevin looked up at Jo in the booth and she smiled down at him. He lowered his eyes, smiling at the ground.

Zarina caught the exchange.

"I don't mean to be nosy," she began. "And it's certainly none of my business... but..."

"Yes?" asked Jo. "Is there something you wanted to ask me?"

Zarina looked at her, trying to read her tone. Jo was an interesting character. The two women had been business partners for less than a year. They'd met in the most random of circumstances. Jo had been in Keytown for a teachers' conference and come into Zoomdweebies coffee shop. The two had struck up a conversation that turned into a debate about women and porn. They'd ended up exchanging email addresses and keeping in touch over social media and a "what if" conversation about starting a classy, sexy website for women had become a series of meet-ups and coffees and planning sessions and eventually blossomed into VXD Enterprises. It was an investment of time and labor and money. They'd become friends in the process, but essentially they were business partners first.

Jo laughed. "You're going to ask me about Kevin."

"I don't need to ask you about Kevin if you don't want

me to," said Zarina, ever the laid-back chick in the room. She pulled her long black hair into a ponytail so she'd have something to do with her hands. She adjusted her glasses on the end of her nose, unnecessarily. Her dark eyes barely hid the twinkle.

"Oh my God, will you stop fidgeting," said Jo, play-slapping at Zarina's hand. "Look, it's no big deal. I mean I think I might have a little crush on our director, that's all."

"That's all, huh?" said Zarina, giving Jo a playful nod. "OK, then. Moving on. I declare this business meeting a success."

"Yes, I don't think we can continue to discuss search engine optimization while these four gentlemen are about to get assless chaps put on them, do you?" asked Jo playfully.

"Not with straight faces," said Zarina. "I'm just the webmaster. I'll leave the other master stuff up to you!"

"Oh, come on," said Jo. "One of these days, I'm going to get you down to the dungeon to try out some of the gear just for fun."

Zarina's naturally olive complexion instantly turned a pasty white.

"If I was really honest with myself I would admit I've been curious at times," Zarina replied. "I used to joke that the words 'dungeon' and 'fun' didn't belong in the same sentence, but I've put so many videos on the website that I've wondered a few times....what it might be like, or what it might feel like to try…"

Her face blushed as she looked at Jo, and suddenly she felt

self-conscious around her much more confident partner.

Jo laughed heartily. "Whoa, down, girl. I'm certainly not going to drag you down to the dungeon and make you my sex slave against your will. But anytime you'd like to come down and play, you just let me know."

Zarina looked at her, then glanced down at the filming room floor, where things were swinging into high gear. The actresses had been given final touches with hair and makeup by the local cosmetology school student who was talented but not overpriced. The four actors had received thin coatings of coconut oil, which gave them attractive muscular sheens on camera without making them "too slippery" for applying punishment and bondage equipment. The lighting assistant, currently majoring in theatre at the local community college, who had learned the skill during dozens of community theatre productions, also talented but inexpensive, had adjusted the spotlights *again* while silently cursing the daylight for inconsistently fading in and out (*these damn storms, coming and going*, he'd complained, *how the fuck am I supposed to run these lights when the natural light won't stay the same for five fucking seconds?*).

"I do love to watch," Zarina said. "And actually my husband, Stanley, also loves to watch later the same evening we film. Your 'scary' dungeon is hot as hell from my perch up here in this glass room, Jo."

"I don't think anyone who experiences it thinks my dungeon is truly scary," said Jo. "Especially the satisfied clients who spend a great deal of money to spend private session time there with me."

"You mean your 'film students' for the purposes of our VXD Enterprises business, of course," said Zarina, winking at her.

"Of course," said Jo. "I'm a teacher, after all."

"I know they learn a great deal from you during class time," said Zarina.

"You're damn straight they do," said Jo. She walked over to Zarina, passing behind her in the control booth, and brushed one single finger across Zarina's right wrist, where it was resting on the control panel, for the briefest of seconds. It could have seemed like an accident, but both women knew it was not. "So keep my invitation to the dungeon in mind, business partner, in case you are ever interested in learning a little bit more about that aspect of how the business is run."

Zarina could feel the shiver start in her wrist and run straight up her arm and down her neck to her nipples, which immediately responded by hardening ever slightly. She took in a breath, swallowing hard. She couldn't believe Jo had such a magnetic effect on everything she touched.

Jo picked up a headset from the hook above the control panel so she could communicate with Kevin on the filming floor.

"Are you ready for some music down there, Mr. Executive Director?" asked Jo.

"Yes, ma'am," he responded. "That is, yes, Madame

Executive Producer."

Jo used the main sound controls and turned on music that wouldn't be heard on the film but that the actors could hear as they got ready to begin filming: "Sadeness" by Enigma.

Jo sat down. It went against everything in her nature as a dominatrix to let Kevin take control of the scene below her. As far as Zarina knew, she was a dominatrix for fun, for filming, for show. As what was referred to as a true "vanilla," Zarina had no idea of the extent of the dominant-submissive lifestyle.

Jo had been a dominatrix since she discovered that the lifestyle existed — since high school. She'd been a movie junkie; she'd seen *9 1/2 Weeks* and gone looking for less-famous yet very powerful movies like *Secretary* and *The Piano Teacher*, but it was her college literature minor that led her to explore (outside the classroom, of course) the works of Bataille and Masoch and their examinations of pleasure and pain. She was bothered by some of the anti-feminist messages in the works, though she tried to attribute them to the time periods in which they were written. She always wished she could find more works written by women — she'd devoured everything ever written by Anais Nin and longed for more.

She glanced down to the film set, to these part-time actresses who knew nothing about the true meaning of the domme-sub lifestyle. It didn't matter. They weren't here for that. The website was for entertainment. Clients who came to her privately — not Kevin, he was a plaything, really a little project she'd taken on just for her own pleasure and fun, whom she happened to have developed some feelings for, despite her normal policies — did so because they needed and respected that world. Not because they saw Fifty Shades of whatever a few years back and they wanted to be tied up. That wasn't even close to what this world was all about. Cute neckties and "oh my"? Not quite.

Pleasure that comes from pain is *real*, Jo thought as she looked down at the women attaching the heavy handcuffs to the men, who looked bored. People who give pain and people who seek it find each other like creeks find rivers and rivers find oceans; they just *do*. The websites and the clubs are there and people form relationships not by virgins stumbling into billionaires' offices, but because they carefully select one another through very rigorous screening processes. They sign detailed contracts. Jo was here to provide them because they *trusted her* and they trusted one another, they sought and found one another out of a deep and abiding need for these dominant-submissive relationships that went deep into their psyches, into *who they were* because they had discovered it was how they found their release and passion.

Kevin had never been a submissive before. He took to it naturally and he seemed very, very happy in the role; a natural. This was something he'd needed his whole life and hadn't even known it. She looked at him now. He brushed a hand haphazardly through that sexy salt-and-pepper hair as he pointed out the camera angle he wanted to the camerawoman. His brows were furrowed in concentration and his white linen shirt was slightly wrinkled. She felt her own body respond to him; her nipples stiffened slightly and she felt a longing rush to the center of her thighs as she thought of their many hours of pleasure together, and she sat up straight, fighting off the images. It was odd to see him in control. That was her role. She bit her lip, hard, to stop herself from getting on the headset or physically going down the steps to take charge of the scene before her, but it literally was not her job and she knew that as a true leader, she would let her employee do his work or risk affecting the outcome.

She was pleased to see the actresses engaged in a heavy make-out session; she hadn't known they were a couple, or hell, for all she knew, they had just been bored waiting. Either way, they were getting themselves "fluffed up" for the scene. One of the men was watching his phone and masturbating, common prep for a scene. Two of the guys were watching the women and the fourth guy was busy getting locked into position at the ankles. Kevin was telling them "two minutes" and it looked like they were about to have a pretty good show, even though the lighting guy was making adjustments and whining again about the cloudy sky; natural light through those high windows was always better.

Suddenly a call came into to the control room. It was Lorena, the producer.

"Uh, Houston, we have a problem," said Lorena, who also happened to be a psychic when she wasn't filming fetish orgy bondage scenes for Vixenden.club.

"What's up, Lorena?" asked Jo into her mic. She looked down at the filming room floor trying to visually find what the problem might be.

"It's Abu," said Lorena, who had walked over to a corner of the filming room floor and was speaking softly into her headset so as not to be overhead. "He's meowing again. I told you I had a bad feeling about this guy the first day he came in here with the meowing."

"Oh no," said Zarina. "Lorena is never wrong about anyone. She warned us about this Abu guy, that he was going to get freaky."

"Oh, for fuck's sake," said Jo. "Kevin, could you come up to the booth please?"

"Of course, Jo," said Kevin through his headset. She watched him immediately hustle upstairs.

Jo and Zarina watched as Lorena returned to the set and to the tall, handcuffed man at one corner of the bed.

"Kevin, what is this guy's deal? We've talked about this before!" said Jo. "Can we get him under control?"

"Oh my God, he brought his silk bag, and he has the anal beads out again," said Zarina.

"Look, he's the best guy we have in scenes sex-wise," said Kevin, "he's hot on film, once we can get him settled down. But you know he has this anal cat fetish thing, and we just need to get past that."

"And he doesn't speak any English," said Jo. "How did we even end up with Abu the meowing cat anal fetish guy?

Someone remind me. Jesus."

Zarina and Kevin looked at each other, knowing laughter would be an appropriate response to that question in literally any other scenario in the universe, but they didn't want to risk Jo raging at them, especially with an entire scene about to be filmed downstairs, so they looked down, avoiding additional eye contact and fighting the urge to break into hysterics.

"I think the thing to do is just let him have one of his toys," said Kevin. "That's worked in the past and it won't affect the scene, and it usually stops the meowing."

"That sounds like a good idea," said Zarina, "and it will get the production underway again quickly with the least amount of hassle."

"MEOWWRGGHHMEOOOOWWWW!!!" said Abu, dressed in nothing but his shackled ankle cuffs, from below them on the filming room floor. His coconut-oiled prick stood at straight attention, and he waved his red white and blue anal beads around in the air like he was about to lasso the bull at the rodeo.

Lorena threw her hands skyward in the direction of the control booth. The other actors exhibited a range of emotions — from shock (two hadn't done a scene with Abu before) to annoyance and eye rolls (two had) to helpfulness — one actress simply grabbed the anal beads and raised her hand, a gesture of gracious voluntarism. "Could we just shove the damn thing up his ass so we can shut him the fuck up, get to work, and get home sometime today?"

"Go for it," said Jo over the loudspeaker system. "Candy to the rescue, everyone. Let's get started."

"*Meow*," said Abu, quietly.

Lorena shook her head, headed back to her filming position. "We can only hope someone listens to me about the hurricane we have coming at the end of this summer," she told Jo through her microphone, "but probably no one will. Day in the life of a damn psychic. *We know* and *we tell you* and still no one listens."

Kevin looked at Jo and Zarina with a smile and said, "I remember when I was a Naval Academy pilot," and walked downstairs to the film set.

"I'm a goddamn kindergarten teacher," said Jo, shaking her head. "I could be cutting out the alphabet in primary colors right now."

"I own a coffee shop," said Zarina with a smile. "But we just have to laugh."

"Or we'll all go mad," said Jo. "Maybe we should think about making a special fetish video starring Assbu next time."

Chapter 6

Jeannie Appleton sat at the dining room table of her home at 101 Oak Street in Stony Mill, Keytown, with a sick feeling growing in the pit of her stomach. She tried to sip her English breakfast tea, but it tasted bitter despite the agave nectar. She looked around at her Pier One Imports decorations, admiring the job that the cleaning service had done. This home had once been a source of such pride for her. She strove for perfection in her life in all things. Her children's grades, their athletic achievements, their extracurricular activities, her involvement with the PTA, and yes, her husband's presidency of their subdivision's homeowners association… those were all things that very much *meant something to her*. Now, the shades and curtains were all drawn in the windows around the house, and she hid from the life that had once seemed so perfect before sex club scandals and "scarlet letter society" bloggers had torn all of that apart.

Her children, CJ and Kaylah, were currently attending

their last week of the school year. There was a knock at the front door. She rose, knowing it was her husband, Chaz. She felt a bizarre sense of pleasure at the fact that he had to knock at his own door. She walked to the door and opened it. He stood there, flanked by two attorneys, hers and his. She looked at the attorneys and said, "I'd like to speak with my soon-to-be-ex-husband for a moment. Would you two gentlemen mind waiting in the kitchen?"

"Of course, Mrs. Appleton," said J. P. Fitzklein III of the downtown law firm of Dean, Brucefeld and Fitzklein, who represented Chaz Appleton and had negotiated his bail and prison release on the white-collar charges of embezzlement from the homeowners association. The HOA had collectively decided that he was no good to them in jail, where he couldn't repay the $167,348.92 he currently owed them. The court had ordered a repayment system and his landscaping company was worth more to them with him running it outside the prison system.

Jeannie's attorney, Gregory Dennis, smiled at her briefly and nodded his agreement.

"If you need me, Jeann—er, Mrs. Appleton, I'll be right in here," he said.

"You know I prefer Jeannie at this point, Greg," she said, with a tight-lipped smile. "Thank you."

She closed the double glass doors to the dining room behind Chaz, who had pulled out a polished mahogany dining room chair and sat himself down. She sat across from him, cocking her head slightly to the side, looking at him as if he were a particularly odd-looking specimen on a tray at a science lab. Disgusting, but nonetheless necessary to analyze.

"How does it feel not to even be allowed inside your own home without being accompanied by a team of attorneys?" asked Jeannie. "And that's only because I said I didn't want the cop cars out front this time."

Chaz smiled at her. "Look, Jeannie, I've been as humiliated as I can be through this whole thing. I got caught at a sex club. I got caught taking money from the pot to try to make ends meet to keep you in the certain lifestyle you'd come to demand and expect. I lost my home and my family and my hockey league and my friends. What the hell more do you want from me?"

"Don't you dare try to blame me for your miserable indiscretions with women and crime," said Jeannie, slamming down her tea cup into its antique saucer, her face turning bright red. "I have to take my children to camp and to school and sports in this community and face the stares and laughter and humiliation that you have caused us. It was front page news for weeks! I would have loved to never return to this town again, but I had no choice. I couldn't take the children away from everything they knew. So now I have to lower my head in embarrassment over *your* shameful acts and sins! I have to drive thirty minutes to take our kids to a church in a different town on Sundays! And then I have to drive into this neighborhood with the nickname of 'Stony Pill.' It's positively horrifying."

"Jeannie, look, I'm sorry," said Chaz. "I don't know if that even helps you to hear me say it but I am. I'm living in a one-bedroom apartment, I'm trying to save my company, I'm doing everything the judge says I need to do so that I can have my visits with the kids. I really don't know what else to say or do."

Jeannie lowered her teacup more gently this time, responding to his apology. She placed the cup and saucer down on the dining room table, smoothing her skirt and trying to smooth her jangled nerves. Her neat brown bob and yellow cardigan twinset, her perfect-on-the-outside appearance, hadn't been affected by the scandal that had swarmed around her for months. Keeping up appearances had simply been what she'd always done. But her insides were a wreck. She was taking antidepressants, sleeping pills, and a prescription antacid. She remained the PTA president regardless of how mortifying her husband's demise had been. This was the first time she had heard him apologize, and as she looked over at him, she realized how undone he had become. He was disheveled; his ragged sweatpants, unshaven face, and wrinkled T-shirt reflected a complete lack of care. His hair hadn't been cut, and there were dark circles under his eyes.

And yet still she felt no sympathy for him. His poor choices had ruined their lives.

"You need to take better care of yourself," she said, standing. "You look like a homeless person, and when my children are in your care in the future I will not have them see you or be seen with you looking like that. They will be home from school shortly and you may visit with them while your attorney is here. My attorney and I will be in another room while you are here."

She turned on the heel of one low black pump and left the room, closing the glass French door behind her. She dismissed Mr. Fitzklein to the dining room to accompany his client during the visitation with the children after commenting on his client's appearance as though he were somehow responsible for it. She then turned to her attorney and invited him to sit down in the more comfortable living room.

"The children won't be here for another half hour," said Jeannie, clearly upset, to Greg. "I can't really even stand being here in this building with him for that long."

Greg Dennis looked at Jeannie from behind his black designer glasses. "Jeannie, you don't need to be here at the house during the visitation if you don't want to. We could take a ride over to my office if you'd like, or just go get some coffee. There's no reason for you to be stressed."

"But I don't like the idea of him being here with the kids…" began Jeannie. She looked at her attorney. For these past months of the stress and the tears and the agony, he had been such a solid rock of wisdom and empathy. He'd gone above and beyond the call of duty, often coming to the house after business hours to answer questions or bring paperwork so she didn't have to bring the kids to his downtown office.

The truth was, she had developed an enormous crush on him that she knew was inappropriate and unprofessional.

"I trust Jerry," said Greg, calmly, his broadcaster-quality voice having a soothing, reassuring effect on her. "We've worked together on dozens of cases over the years, and as long as he's here with Chaz and the kids nothing's going to happen. Also, Chaz has never been any kind of flight risk."

"That's true," said Jeannie. "It's not like he has any money to go anywhere."

"As you know, the court controls all his money," said Greg, smiling. "Let's get you out of here."

He lightly touched her arm. She felt a shiver run from the point of contact up her sleeve, through the fabric of her sweater, into her flesh, and straight to the center of her body. It made her feel more alive than she had ever remembered. Certainly than she could ever remember feeling with Chaz, at least in many years. She struggled not to visibly tremble, or draw her arm away. She just wasn't used to being touched. By anyone. *Ever.*

Greg took the other attorney aside and explained they would return in an hour, after Chaz's visit with the kids. Greg and Jeannie walked down the driveway past the Mercedes that Chaz and his attorney had arrived in, to the BMW that belonged to Greg.

As she climbed into the car, Jeannie tried to collect herself. She had tried to explain away the feelings she was having for Greg as some sort of "teacher crush," a simple schoolgirl-style fantasy that had begun because he was in a position of authority; he'd been so helpful to her in a desperate situation. Her husband had cheated on her, lied to her, joined a secret swingers' club in their own neighborhood where he was the very homeowners association president, and then to add insult to injury, embezzled from the organization he was running. And Greg, whose downtown office she had sat in on that rainy day those months ago, crying, had been there to comfort her. *Doing his job*, she reminded herself.

But she hadn't been able to help noticing the office photos he kept of his kids, but none in sight of a wife. No ring. She had tried but been unable to avoid his glances that seemed to linger for a beat too long. She knew they must be her imagination. She hadn't been attracted to a man since she met her husband so many years ago, and certainly hadn't been able to imagine herself as attractive to a man since then either. Those feelings were so foreign to her, especially in the swamp-like emotional despair she had felt surrounded in for so long now in her life. She couldn't even remember the last time Chaz had made love to her — was it six months ago? Eight?

"Would that be OK? Jeannie?" Greg was looking at her with concern, now stopped at the stop sign, about to pull out of the neighborhood. She'd been completely lost in her thoughts. "Are you all right?"

"I'm so sorry," said Jeannie. "I just lost my train of thought. What was it you asked me?"

"I just asked if you might like to stop at that old place over on Frederick Street and get a milkshake or something," said Greg. "It's across from the park and I thought maybe you looked like you could use some fresh air."

"A milkshake?" Jeannie asked, somewhat bewildered. She vaguely remembered the old '50s-style ice cream shop from years before, but she didn't think she'd been there since high school. She had no idea it was even still open. It had never even occurred to her to take her kids there. It was in the old part of town, so far removed from the suburban strip malls and shopping areas they were used to around town.

Greg laughed. "It's a drink, made from ice cream and milk."

Jeannie smiled. She actually felt the effort it took in the muscles in her face to do this. She raised her hand to her cheek.

"What is it?" asked Greg.

Tears nearly sprung to the brims of Jeannie's eyes and she quickly pressed hard at the corners of her eyes to fight them back.

"It's nothing," she said, pulling herself back together. "I was just thinking that it's sad I don't smile more, for my children's sake. And that they've never been to the milkshake shop."

"Well, let's try it out, and maybe you can bring them back here next time if you like it," said Greg. "Or we could even bring back some milkshakes for them with us when we return to the house."

She stole a brief glance over at him, his sandy blond

curls, the easy way he held the steering wheel, admiring his confidence, the ease with which he seemed to handle the world. She unclenched her hands from the edges of her seat, tried to sit back in her leather seat more comfortably, exhaled. Something about being around Greg made her realize what a very tightly wound ball of yarn she was, how much she disliked this about herself.

"Yes, a milkshake sounds perfect," Jeannie said. She looked out the window. She couldn't remember the last time she was a passenger in a car, and not the driver.

They drove the short few miles across town. Greg turned left into the one-story white diner-style ice cream shop. It was exactly as Jeannie remembered it, frozen in time. It was like she'd been transported in a time capsule back to her childhood.

Before she knew it, Greg had walked to her side of the car and opened the BMW's door for her. She felt like the theme song for *Happy Days* was going to start playing. She actually felt the heat, the color rise to her cheeks. If she hadn't just climbed out of a very modern car and he hadn't been wearing a very modern dark gray suit, she would've sworn she was currently in 1956. They walked toward the old-fashioned lettering on the sign above the take-out window. He ordered a chocolate malt, opting against the whipped cream and cherry, and she selected a vanilla milkshake.

"I don't remember the last time I had a homemade milkshake with real ice cream," said Jeannie. "I don't usually let the kids have so much sugar. Maybe Greek yogurt..."

Greg laughed. "I get it. My ex-wife used to be the same way, with the sugar and the dyes and the high fructose corn syrup and all that. No offense, of course, whatever's good for the kids. But I bring my kids here and let them get whatever they want. I would've loved to have had a place like this as a kid way out in the sticks!"

Jeannie took in the information, not wanting to be nosy and ask for more information about his children, and took two straws from the dispenser.

"There's really nothing wrong with ice cream," she offered, with a weak smile.

"Of course not!" he said. He paid for the milkshakes. "Listen, would you like to take a walk on the path across the street here? This old playground is great. They haven't replaced it with all that safety equipment yet so it still has the old dangerous metal stuff from when we were kids."

"Oh my gosh, I remember it," said Jeannie. "I can't believe it's still here. We don't have a whole lot of time, but maybe just for a little while."

They walked. It was starting to get dark. The playground was a bit overgrown. Jeannie couldn't help but wonder who was in charge of maintaining it. The City of Keytown didn't seem to have it as part of their recreation department system, or it would've been updated with new equipment long before now. It wasn't close enough to any community, or it would've been kept up by them. It seemed to be a recreational anomaly, a leftover from a bygone era, not unlike the ice cream shop.

Lucky enough to have escaped the passage of time with no one seeming to notice and give it an unnecessary "upgrade," she couldn't help but think. She was torn between her reaction to this place as a responsible, safety-aware adult, and a woman who was once, long ago, so many years ago she could hardly remember, a child at this playground.

The playground equipment had thick steel pipe frames with rusty chains holding up the creaky swings that moved slightly in the breeze, one side of one swing now hanging loose. The merry-go-round had potential splinter-giving wooden slats for seats that would've been ripped out by any modern parents in their right minds. The large monkey bar half-moon piece would never be put in today—it was rusty, slippery, and the fall from its highest point would potentially cause a broken limb. A high metal sliding board featured a dangerous spinning descent that would've been very hot in summer and could cause very dangerous falls from any height. As a PTA president, Jeannie looked around in horror at all the potential injuries and lawsuits (*didn't Greg see all these potential lawsuits?!* Jeannie wondered) that could happen on the playground.

"Isn't this place great?!" asked Greg, smiling like a little kid. "Just like when we were kids!" With a running start, he grabbed one of the metal handles of the merry-go-round and jumped up, letting it carry him around a few times, jumping off effortlessly, still holding his malted milkshake with the other hand.

Jeannie stood looking at him, surprised once again at her reaction. He was, after all, the lawyer here. She took a sip of her milkshake and sighed.

He walked over to her and motioned to the swing. "Want a push?"

She looked at the rusted, creaky swing and up at him. As he'd walked past, she'd gotten a whiff of whatever it was that he smelled like — something spicy and manly and like nothing Chaz had ever remotely smelled like. She wanted him to just keep standing there. She sipped too loudly from her milkshake, slurping, and he laughed.

"Loving that milkshake after all, huh?" Greg asked.

"I feel like we should get back to the kids?" asked Jeannie.

Greg looked at his watch. "Well, we have thirty more minutes. You don't look too thrilled about the swing. How about this amazing sliding board?" He tossed his sandy blond curls in the direction of the tall metal structure.

And she melted. His smile undid her. For months she had been wanting nothing more than to be alone with him, and now here he was — no office, no kids around, no paperwork. Milkshakes and playgrounds. She felt like a kid. She tried to let herself feel like a kid.

"Sure," Jeannie found herself saying. "Let's go down the slide. Even though I'm wearing these." She looked down at her low black pumps.

"We'll take great care ascending you to the top of this here tower, m'lady," said Greg playfully, bowing before her formally as though he was some sort of medieval servant, and she laughed. *What an amazing feeling that was*, she thought. *Laughing.*

She walked nervously to the slide. She was sure she hadn't been down a sliding board in thirty years. She left her pumps in the grass right beside the steps to the sliding board, taking the first step up, and stood in her stocking feet on the first metal step, looking up toward the top of the metal slide, suddenly afraid of the height.

"I'll be right behind you, fair lady, fear not!" Greg said in his new fake knight-in-shining-armor voice. He placed their milkshakes on a nearby bench.

Jeannie pushed aside thoughts of how, as she walked up the steps of the slide, Greg was going to able to see directly up her skirt! She was wearing bicycle short-style pantyhose, thank goodness!

She got up three steps and paused, thinking once again that she couldn't believe how high they'd built this thing—*for children!* The steps were so narrow. She looked up, thinking how high she'd be by the time she got to the top. She tried not to think of the germs on the rusty metal, she tried not to think of falling. Whimsical, spontaneous playground gallivanting was exactly the opposite of her nature.

Seeming to read her thoughts, Greg said, "Jeannie, it's a sliding board. You can do this." Leaving his business shoes in the grass below, he took a step so he was one rung below her.

She could feel the heat of him below her. She liked it. In

spite of herself, she liked the feeling of needing his help. She had run her family, and the school, and the neighborhood because her husband had been such an imbecile for so long. What she needed or what she might enjoy, not to mention what might be *fun*, had not been a consideration in her life since she could remember — maybe ever. What an odd thought.

"I — I need your help," stammered Jeannie, "Could you... stay near me?"

"Of course, fair maiden," Greg answered in his medieval impersonation, "what kind of protector of the law would I be if I were not to see about the safety of her ladyship?"

Jeannie took a step toward the top and Greg took a step to follow her, placing one hand around her waist and the other on the metal handle next to hers. One socked foot rested beside her stockinged one in turn as they finished the flight of steps.

As she reached the top, where a small iron grate landing area allowed them both to stand before descending the twisting metal slide, he stood directly beside her, and she turned to face him. She steadied herself by holding at first onto the metal handle, gripping it with all her might, but she had to lean slightly to do this. He took one of her hands. She looked at him. Taking his hands meant standing at a very tall height and letting go of the structure. She would have to trust him.

She felt the early summer breeze rush through her trademark perfectly kept bob, thinking it must be a mess, and for once she didn't care.

"Thank you," she said, and she proceeded to reach her hands around that messy blond head of her attorney and do the most spontaneous thing she'd ever done in her life. She pulled his face toward hers and kissed his smiling, full sexy lips even as he tried to answer her. She could feel him hesitate for a moment, but then she felt the softness, the taste of the surrender in his lips.

She felt something else as he pulled her closer to him, letting fall the veil of professionalism he may have tried to hold onto in that moment. She'd known on some level, hoped at least, that he wanted her. But she hadn't been positive. All those meetings over all these months... the stolen glances, the extra time in meetings—what she hoped was a flirtation. She hadn't been sure, and it had been so long since anyone had paid any attention to her, but she had hoped so hard. And now, she knew she had been right.

Neither of them seemed to care, had even looked around to see if anyone was looking at the middle-aged couple standing on the metal platform at the top of the worn, metal slide, its paint faded, atop the abandoned, overgrown playground in the park across from the old ice cream shop at the far end of town.

They moved against each other, his business suit pressing against her skirt, until she eventually slid downward, backward, her knees slowly buckling sideways toward the metal platform, as if she were melting.

"W-what are we doing?" Jeannie asked, feeling the cold metal against the back of her pantyhose as the cotton of her skirt landed haphazardly askew.

Greg answered her with a firm kiss. "You started this, fair maiden," he answered. "Your wish is my command. I merely delivered you safely to the top of your tower."

For a fleeting moment, Jeannie had the most ridiculous thought, about a song on the radio. Her daughter had begun singing it, and Jeannie had made her change the station. Something about *"My milkshake brings all the boys to the yard..."*

She couldn't help but smile, even as she found herself pressing her skirt upward against the insistent bulge she felt beneath Greg's belt. She moved against it ever so slightly, and kissed him again. She didn't want to go down the slide. She wanted to stay right here. She didn't care if every member of the PTA, the school board, every teacher, parent, the entire school population and the citizenry of Keytown joined hands together and said the pledge of allegiance below them on the abandoned playground. She was staying right where she was at this very moment, crumpled skirt, messed up hair, shoes on the ground, and gorgeous, horny, sexy attorney on top of her, grinding against her at the top of a rusty sliding board in a public playground. Maybe that's what came from having already been humiliated in the newspapers by your husband, but she just didn't give a flying fuck anymore. When you didn't have anything to lose, what was there really to care about anymore? Other than her children, of course. *Who she really should be getting back home to....*

For once, for possibly the first time in her life, she pushed thoughts of her kids aside and let her own pleasure come first.

She felt the summer breeze move through the holes in the metal grate of the platform beneath her, moving up her skirt to her already-aroused thighs; their center. Greg's right hand had pushed up her skirt further, and was caressing the underside of her ass, and it felt so, so good and she wanted his hands on her naked body but of course they weren't going to take their clothes off in a public place. Jeannie's left hand played with his blond curls; she raked her fingers through his hair and caressed his neck as her right hand found itself pulling his right ass cheek closer to her—she couldn't help herself from pressing him closer to her. The sensation of his erection, even through the fabric of their clothes, was more pleasure than she had felt in years. Her own husband had been completely vacant in that department for so, so long and now she was desperately hungry for the long-ignored sensation to be satisfied.

She was pleased at the way Greg responded perfectly to her, gently rolling his hips against her, applying the perfect amount of pressure to her aching need as he gently searched her mouth with his tongue. He was rock hard for her and she could feel it all, even through his Armani pants. With one thumb, he explored inside the thin cashmere of her sweater and across the outside of her satiny bra. Her already-aroused breast stiffened in response; she sighed softly.

Within moments, she grabbed on to his belt with her left hand, using her right hand to pull his ass closer to her pulsing, throbbing need, arching her lower back and rolling her hips to meet his slow, rhythmic movements. After only a few more moments of this intense grinding, she cried out, her entire body shivering in an unexpected orgasm that she felt reverberate throughout her entire being. She groaned loudly, unable to stop herself from emitting the primeval sound as the pleasure rocked her body. She lowered herself to the playground metal, shivering in small convulsion-like movements.

"Are you OK?" Greg asked, genuinely concerned. He chuckled softly, not wanting to appear to laugh, but slightly amused at her dramatic orgasm. "I don't think I've ever seen a woman respond quite so... enthusiastically to me without me even having to take any of our clothes off!"

Jeannie was breathless. "I—I, I don't, I've ... it's been a very long time since I... I don't even know if I've ever... quite like that..." she panted. Her face was completely flushed as she tried to catch her breath. She suddenly raised her head, looking around the playground.

"Oh my gosh, I'm so sorry, I..." Jeannie began.

Greg grinned at her. "I don't think we have an audience." He laughed. "Though it's kind of a shame. We made for a pretty impressive show."

Jeannie's breath had slowed but was still quickened. "We would be arrested... for public..."

Greg chuckled again. "I could get us off." He laughed again, from the bottom of his belly. "Well, there's a double entendre for you."

He helped Jeannie up to a sitting position.

"We haven't even taken the ride yet! Let's get you down this slide and back to your children, m'lady," he said valiantly.

"I'm sure we should talk about what just..." began Jeannie.

"We should," said Greg, "and we will. But let's get our shoes back on, and get our milkshakes back, and get inside the car, and we can discuss everything then."

He suddenly grabbed the metal bar that crossed above the slide, screamed "WHEEEEEE!!!" and descended the twisted, turning metal side all the way to the bottom.

"OK, I'm here ready to catch you," said Greg. "Your turn."

Jeannie smiled at the top, less afraid now.

She pointed her stockinged feet out before her, dangling over the edge, and she let go, laughing all the way to the bottom.

"That," she said, "was a really fun ride."

Chapter 7

Once known as the Keytown Mouse, Rachel Tisdale was freshly out of rehab for a prescription drug addiction to her son's Adderall. She was lucky her husband, Martin, had pulled some strings, finding her an attorney who had landed her here instead of in jail on charges of buying illegal prescription drugs at the suburban swingers' club in her neighborhood, especially after they'd found out she'd also been selling them to a few moms in Stony Mill.

Now living on Matthew's Island with her sister, Rachel got off her bike and walked into the Matthew's Island Country Store wearing a baseball hat over her moppy red ginger curls and sunglasses. She appreciated the fact that she was still anonymous on the island. She greeted Patty and Jack, the store's friendly owners, who told her about the day's specials, the freshly baked items Patty had just made and the wine specials that were going to be featured that week at the Friday wine tasting. When a new person showed up on the island,

Patty was curious about where they came from, but it was never polite to ask. Eventually, on a small island like this, the stories all got told sooner or later.

Since Rachel had been out of rehab, she was staying at her sister's small apartment. It wasn't ideal, but Martin had insisted he wanted a divorce and had initiated court proceedings in an effort to keep her from seeing her son, Jacob. She only had limited visitation rights at the moment because of her prescription drug abuse charges after the whole Keytown Swingers' Club arrest fiasco. In some ways she missed the simplicity of her days sitting at an accounting desk writing about the Scarlet Letter Society and a fancy finished basement full of people sleeping with other people's spouses. But now, she really didn't want to go back to that town again except for the visits to see her teenager Jacob, who acted embarrassed to see his mother.

Rachel, now officially legally separated, got a check in the mail each month from Martin that paid for her living expenses. When her nine-dollar double cheeseburger and fries and a soda special arrived in its brown paper package, she paid for it along with a few snacks (she'd put on some weight since she left rehab), small household items, and a slice of Patty's banana walnut cake. She looked at the wall of small bottles of liquor and it took all her will to ignore them, as it did Patty's invite to the wine tasting. She would give anything for a bottle of wine or a few shots of booze, but even though she was in recovery for an Adderall addiction, she was supposed to stay clean from all substances. She thanked Jack, who rang up her order, put her sunglasses back on, and walked toward the door and her bike. Just as she walked out the door, someone familiar walked into the store past her, chatting with another woman she didn't recognize.

It took her a moment to recognize someone completely out of context—like when you see the dentist at the grocery store in plain clothes, or your child's teacher at a movie theatre. She thought about it for another moment while she put her sandwich in the bike's basket, and then it dawned on her. *Zarina, the coffee shop owner at Zoomdweebies in Keytown? What on earth would she be doing on Matthew's Island on a weekday afternoon?*

Not wanting to be recognized, she rode her bike down the street, wondering who the other woman was. She definitely hadn't recognized her from Keytown. Curiosity, as it always had in her life, got the best of her. Rachel was convinced she looked like ninety-eight percent of the women on the island if she was riding on the side of the road wearing an old cotton sundress and a baseball hat and sunglasses, so she rode around in a large circle past the Cattail Harbor Marina, waiting for Zarina and her friend to come out. It was only a three-mile-long island, and she could easily see where they went from here.

I have been so bored and miserable on this island for the last three weeks, Rachel thought, *this is the most exciting thing that's happened to me. Might as well stick around and follow the action.*

Rachel's younger sister Sandy worked at Walmart in the nearby city of Easton. Her boyfriend, Tyler, ran a small fishing boat out of the marina but Rachel was suspicious that he made money selling something other than fish, crabs, and oysters. He didn't seem to spend much time on the boat and Rachel thought it was awkward how much time she had to spend with him alone in the apartment. He was ten years younger than she was and Sandy was at work a lot of the time. Rachel was supposed to be "in recovery" and spending her time at meetings, but she didn't even have a car.

"You can drive me to work when you need my car," said Sandy. "I told you I don't mind."

At thirty-three, the freckle-faced blond younger sister had been ever-loyal to her older sister. Rachel was so humiliated to have to impose herself into her younger sister's life. She felt sick watching her little sister work these late shifts six days a week to support Tyler the alleged waterman.

"Honey, I can't get up at three a.m. to drive an hour and a half like that," said Rachel. "I'm fine to ride a bike to the church for the meeting." And no way in hell was she going to ask Tyler for a ride to anything. He walked around in his white wife-beaters, jeans slung low over his skinny hips, looking like he needed a trip to the dentist, sneering at her about whether she could go to the grocery store or maybe clean the bathroom.

Rachel knew she should be doing something to pitch in, but there just wasn't really anywhere to work on the island.

She'd tried to get a cleaning job at Matthew's Island Inn, but that nightmare of an operation was so fly-by-night there was no telling from day to day who was getting paid or not or whether the place would be open from one minute to the next. She'd waited an hour there before she'd even found anyone to ask about the job, and even then the woman had honestly warned her against even trying to mess around with the place.

Rachel sighed as she circled the marina parking lot, then she came back up the main road and caught a glance of Zarina's long black hair coming out of the country store. Zarina got back into a car that must've belonged to her friend, who was driving. They made a right onto the main road. It was less than half a mile to the drawbridge, so unless they were leaving the island, she'd be able to see which way they turned. She pedaled faster. She could see the car put its left turn signal on. Were they turning into the bait and tackle store? That would be odd, since they just came from the country store. Where else could they possibly be headed? Rachel didn't think there was anything else down that road, but she'd only been on the island a few weeks. She didn't want to follow them, so she turned around near the drawbridge and headed back to the apartment with her lunch. She'd have to investigate what was down the lane past the bait and tackle store another time.

For now she made a left turn and headed down Turkey Neck Road and down the short driveway back to the one-level, two-bedroom apartment she shared with her sister and Tyler. Seeing his beat-up Honda in the driveway, she was disappointed. It hadn't been there when she left so she had been hoping to have her lunch in peace. She parked her bike, walking inside to put down the brown bag of grocery items in the kitchen. She didn't want to go her room and eat the brown bagged lunch on her bed, but if she ate in the combination living-dining area, he'd obviously be there and she hated having to have a conversation with him. There was a small porch off the back, so she decided to take her lunch out there. She had to walk through the small living space to get there.

Tyler was flopped on the couch watching the Kardashians. She tried to walk past him without an exchange, but he started with a charming opener.

"Hey!"

Rachel winced, facing away from him. She hoped she'd make it through the room without interaction. She turned slightly but did not face him, thinking maybe he was just reprimanding her for walking in front of the TV.

"Yeah, Tyler? I was just going to go out and eat my—" Rachel started to answer, raising her brown paper bag slightly. She slowly started walking again, hoping the conversation would not continue.

"What the fuck you in such a hurry for?" asked Tyler.

She hated the creepy tone of his voice. She felt so badly for her sister, and couldn't understand for a second why she was dating this piece of trash. She turned to look at him, and her lunch fell to the floor. There, on the small coffee table, was a metal spoon, a lighter, a piece of very thin nautical rope, a needle, and a small bag of powder.

"What the hell are you doing?" asked Rachel.

"Come have a seat and I'll show you," said Tyler, grinning like the Cheshire cat, which displayed his dental needs.

Rachel was in such complete shock that she slowly walked over and did what she was told—maybe out of a desire to learn exactly what was going on so that she could report it to her sister, and transfixed by the paraphernalia on the table. There was no way in hell Sandy knew about this. She would never tolerate drugs in her house. *Would she?*

Or maybe she sat down on the worn, thin cotton fabric of the blue and mauve floral sofa, despite her disgust for Tyler, because she was an addict. Something deep in her psyche, deeper than all the hours of group therapy and individual therapy and journaling and bullshitting of doctors, far deeper than all of that, had a grip on her. And she wondered what was in that powder, and what it would do to her, just for a few minutes.

"You can't…" Rachel began. "My sister… if she ever knew anything about this. You can't do that in this house." Her pulse had quickened and small droplets of sweat had beaded around the edges of her forehead.

"She don't know nothin'," said Tyler, narrowing his eyes. "And you sure as shit ain't never going to tell her. See, this here is how I make money. I don't make enough from the water. I take my boat out, sure I do. Shit, it's even named fer your sister, the *Lady Sandy*. But that boat usually got more 'n' crabs on it if I wanna make 'nuff money to keep this place up."

As he spoke, he rolled up the sleeve of the ragged, thin flannel shirt he wore over his white tank top to reveal the needle-marked skin of his inner elbow. Within moments, she'd watched his expertise at the routine: he heated a small amount of the powder inside the spoon using the lighter, and pulled it into the needle syringe.

"I jus' bring the islanders what they want," said Tyler, "this here import from the mainland."

When he said "islanders" it sounded like *"all-unndurrs"* to Rachel — everything he said had creepy feel to it, enhanced by the grin featuring his half-rotten teeth. She wondered again how her sister had gotten involved with this guy. She thought back to their youth. Her sister had dragged home every injured bird, abandoned rabbit, dead roadkill squirrel to be buried, stray cat, and troubled kid in school home with her. Their father had left their mother for another woman when they were so young, and Sandy was perpetually trying to save something. They'd been so poor, their mother always working at the mall to make ends meet. Sandy must have thought she could save Tyler. It would never happen.

Rachel backed away, toward the furthest corner of the couch, not wanting to see, but seeing. Her breathing picked up its pace. She was horrified and fascinated at the same time. She'd heard that heroin was a common problem among the watermen on the island, had heard many stories at the rehab facility, but she had never seen its use up close before.

She knew her sister would be devastated; that this couldn't continue...

Tyler held the needle poised in the air, filled halfway with its murky amber liquid, and looked directly at her. She stared back into his eyes, drawing her knees up to her chest in an instinctively defensive posture. His eyes were greenish blue and should have been a pretty color, but glazed as they were with drugs and vacant stupidity, they weren't attractive to her in any way.

"*Brown. Fuckin'. Sugar,*" he said to her. "We could be friends, you know. Me and you, just sittin' the fuck around here all the time."

"I don't want to be friends," said Rachel. And suddenly for the strangest reason Lady Gaga echoed in her head. *I don't wanna be friends.*

And suddenly he was way too close to her on the sofa. She could smell his rancid breath, feel his skinny thigh, the denim of his jeans touching her.

"Come on, baby," he said. "You know how they say. First one's on me."

"No," said Rachel. "I'll tell Sandy everything. I can't let this happen. There is no way I can risk everything. I don't want..."

Tyler laughed. "No you ain't gonna tell her nothin. And yes you fuckin' do want."

He snatched the thin nautical rope off the table and whipped it around her arm above the elbow as she tried to fight him off, made a motion to stand up and get away. But her protests weren't fully powered. He pulled her back down, laughing.

"You won't tell her," he said, "because you don't want to. Nah, come on, you just give it a try, and the whole thing is our li'l secret. You ain't gonna tell Sandy a fuckin' thing, and that's the damn end of it. Fair now?"

Rachel's eyes widened as her carrot-top hair spilled out of her baseball cap. Her fist clenched against the rope that had been tied above the bend in her elbow. She knew she was making a huge mistake. Everything she had suffered and lost. But for all the misery her life had become to go away for just a few seconds, didn't she deserve just a quick break from all of it? She closed her eyes.

"Perfect," said Tyler, "look at that beautiful vein."

A flash of guilt about betraying her sister crossed her consciousness. It was similar to the flash of guilt she'd felt when she cheated on her husband, Martin, with the college professor Kate, and of course that hadn't worked out well either. Apparently making life decisions wasn't her forte.

As the liquid rushed into her veins and straight on to her brain, Rachel felt a rush of euphoria that no booze or Adderall had ever come close to bringing her. She had no way of knowing at that moment that her brain's chemistry was forever altered, and if you'd told her, she wouldn't have cared. She also had an odd clarity to her thoughts. *It wasn't that stupid paparazzi song, it was "Bad Romance."*

Like a baby duck will imprint on to the first living thing it sees, Rachel was now unfortunately tied to the disgusting Tyler. But within thirty seconds of the time the needle pricked her skin, all her thoughts were gone and she felt nothing but bliss.

Tyler looked at Rachel lying back on the couch, a half smile on her face. Everything would be different now. She didn't have to worry about a thing.

"Feelin' happy now, aintcha?" he asked.

"Yeah," said Rachel, her head spinning a bit. She managed to formulate one last reasonable, caring thought into a question. "My sister?"

"Nah, she squeaky clean. She ain't usin', I told you she don't know nothing 'bout none of this and it's gon' stay that way. But me and you? We're gon' be good friends now, Rach," said Tyler. "You just wait 'n' see."

Rachel was still in a state of full relaxation when Tyler pulled a used Ruger handgun, slightly rusty from its time on the water in his boat, from the back waistband of his jeans, showed it to her, and placed it on the coffee table.

She was jolted back into a state of awareness, and alarm, and sat up, ready to flee.

"Now, now, none of that," said Tyler. "You ain't gonna need to run. Just like you ain't gonna need to tell Sandy, like I told you before. Only now you understand better why. That gun there ain't for you. It's cuz now you know how I make my money more than crabbin' and oysterin.' I bring fish in on my boat, sure I do, only I bring some other things too. And they're a little more profitable, but I gotta protect myself."

Rachel was too much in shock to speak in answer to Tyler's little speech. It was more words in a row than she'd ever heard him say. She had already felt trapped in this apartment. For the briefest moment, she actually thought about calling her husband in Keytown to come and rescue her off this island, but she was under a "recovery contract" that specified she had to be in the rehab's outpatient program for twelve weeks before she could be considered for full release. A program she of course had just completely violated.

She looked at Tyler, her eyes glassy.

"You look like you need a little rest," said Tyler. "Let's get you to your bedroom now."

Rachel still hadn't spoken. Her eyes flicked to the metal spoon and the needle on the table. Tyler quickly prepared another hit.

"Oh, I see what you's lookin' at," said Tyler. "I knew you was a bad girl the minute I met you. You ain't nothing like your sister. C'mon, up you go."

Tyler took Rachel by the wrist and she stood. Despite herself, all she could think of was when she was going to get the next hit. Because she was an addict, because first the booze and then that stupid Adderall had turned her into one, and because of the power of heroin, that fast, *that damn fast*, she didn't care about her sister. She didn't care about her husband, or even what she had tried to do to get back to her son.

Tyler led her down the hall and she followed him. She followed him no matter how repulsed she'd been by him. She followed him past the tiny guest bedroom that her sister had lovingly prepared for her, buying a bed-in-a-bag set on clearance from Walmart so she would have someplace to stay when she got out of rehab.

Rachel followed Tyler, while he took her by the wrist like a child, to his bedroom door and then he stopped.

"Aw hell, we ain't wanna go in here," said Tyler. "This where me and Sandy go. Let's go 'n' see yer bedroom! Get you all settled in nice and tight fer your rest now! Take a little nap, aight?"

Tyler walked in front of Rachel into the tiny room, outfitted with only a single bed, a nightstand, and a small dresser. He pulled her in, sitting on the bed, patting the spot beside him.

Rachel sat.

"How you feelin' now?" asked Tyler. "Good?"

"I want more," said Rachel.

"Aw, 'course you do, now, don'tcha?" Tyler laughed. "We all do. But you ain't got no money, do ya?"

Rachel looked at him. "How much?"

"You know what?" said Tyler. "I bet you 'n' me, we can work out a little credit arrangement."

He stood up, taking the syringe from out of his back pocket. There was just enough in it for a hit. He knew she'd want more, and that she'd do anything for it.

"Let's you 'n' me play a little game of Simon Says," said Tyler, "like when we was kids. Only it'll be called *Tyler Says*."

Rachel stared at the syringe. She was sweating.

"I'll take that as a yes," said Tyler. "So here we go. Tyler says: *Take off your clothes, and hold out your arm*."

He pulled her by the wrist to a standing position, like she was a marionette puppet.

"I said *Tyler says* now," said Tyler, "so you gotta *do it*."

Rachel blinked; she was under the spell of the heroin. She looked toward the door. There was part of her brain that tried to think about her sister, her sister's house, her sister coming home, the consequences. That part of her brain failed.

She pulled the cotton sundress over her head in a single motion.

"Aw, good girl, now," said Tyler.

Rachel stood in her white bra and white cotton brief panties and put out her arm, licking her lips.

"Aw, no, sugar, you forgot the rest of your clothes," said Tyler. He put down the syringe on the bed, and her eyes followed the drugs. She looked as though she was going to grab the needle, though she had never once injected herself.

"No no no, now," said Tyler, "Tyler didn't say nothin' 'bout grabbin' no needle. Don'tchu go breakin' the rules."

He undid his belt buckle and lowered his jeans and underwear to the floor, picking the needle back up.

"Tyler is just enjoyin' the view," he said. "Now you just take off the rest of them clothes."

Tyler began masturbating, slowly jerking himself off, as Rachel removed the rest of her clothing, sitting back down on the bed, presenting her arm to him. She seemed to be disinterested in what he was doing. He came quickly, making a mess on the floor.

"Aw, see now what you made me do," said Tyler, "that was just too excitin.' Maybe next time we can become even better friends. Here now."

He grabbed her arm, shoving the needle in, and her whole body tensed, waiting for the rush. She had cared about nothing else until then, felt no humiliation, felt nothing but a laser focus on getting the heroin running through her veins. From then on, that's all she would care about. Her life now until its end would be a path where she would trade her recovery, her pride, and her body to her sister's junkie waterman boyfriend in exchange for feeding her brand new heroin addiction.

Chapter 8

Wes and Alfred settled into the charming Bay Room at Sharps Island Inn. They took in the views from the windows. The sunlight shone on the waves of the slightly choppy Chesapeake Bay, though gray clouds were starting to descend.

"Isn't it magnificent?" said Wes. He took off the baseball hat that he wore out of habit to protect his receding hairline from the hot summer sun, combing his salt-and-pepper hair.

"The view is beyond compare," said Alfie. "This combo bridal-baby-shower is just what the doctor ordered for Fourth of July weekend. I was so happy to get out of town."

"I was *lucky* to get out of town. A summer weekend with no production at the theatre is a rare bird," said Wes. "At least no production of ours. The annual ad agency awards ceremony thing is huge, and I *really* should be there, but they convinced me it's been over twenty years that they've been doing it, so they'd be fine without me."

"Yes, dear, the theatre *can* survive without you for one weekend!" said Alfie. He checked his reflection in the mirror, but his Brad-Pitt-lookalike reflection, as usual, needed no adjustment. "Now let's get a cocktail and go take a walk around these gorgeous grounds before the sky opens up and the rains pour down. The forecast is for a storm tonight."

"Fortunately for us the amazing innkeepers Ron and Dale invited us for cocktails on that fabulous porch with all the rocking chairs to watch the sunset," said Wes. "It looks like we will be lucky enough to get to see this sunset before the storm."

"Oh God, well this place just has the best sunsets in the universe, it's like the sun just drops into the water, it is perfectly *stunning*," said Alfie. "Can't wait."

Wes walked over to Alfie and put his arms around him. "It's like we are getting a tiny second honeymoon."

"Amen to that," said Alfie. They kissed one another slowly, deeply. Something about being on Matthew's Island could return romance to any marriage. Theirs had started on the very eve of Maryland's legalization of gay marriage—a snowy mountaintop by candlelight, New Year's Eve, 2012 at midnight.

"We should ask Ron and Dale to renew our vows for us while we are here this weekend," said Wes.

"Well, that's very spontaneous! It *would* be the perfect way to celebrate the Fourth of July weekend," said Alfie. "With a fireworks show at the end! But this weekend is already supposed to be about Maggie and Dave's wedding shower and Eva's baby shower! *And* we didn't bring adorable suits. And there is no shopping anywhere around here. Like *at all*."

"Oh, *divatude*," said Wes, rolling his eyes and kissing his husband on the cheek. He took his hand to lead him downstairs for the sunset cocktail hour. "We don't need adorable outfits to renew our wedding vows right before a fireworks show. And we're not taking away from anyone's anything with a five-minute renewal ceremony. We just need our friends, and some drinks, and shorts and flip-flops. It's about love, it's not a fashion show."

"*Everything* is a fashion show, *ugh*," said Alfie. "Plus we should have *invited people* and gotten a *caterer*, and a *photographer* and had a *DJ*...."

"OK, how about if we just do a very tiny *ce-re-mony*," said Wes, "and then we will have a huge *re-cep-tion par-ty* later, exactly the way you want everything."

"*Yasssssss*," said Alfie, smiling. "I do."

"Let's go have drinks and watch the sunset," said Wes, "and you can tell me all about it."

"And Wes?" said Alfie.

"Yes, baby?" replied Wes.

"That's exactly what I was thinking! Maybe we will have our *baby* by then, and she can be the flower girl, like in a little antique carriage, you know the ones with the four wheels, just *covered* in roses, so she'll be there with us!" said Alfie. He blinked, crinkling up his perfect nose, grinning.

Wes stopped, turning to look into Alfie's gorgeous, ocean-blue eyes. He smiled back at his younger husband, who knew how happy he'd just made him.

"Well, what if our baby is a boy?" he asked, unable to keep the pure joy from his honey brown eyes.

"Well, *duh*, then he's the ring bearer, so he will be in a *boy* carriage with like blue roses or something, and there will be a pillow in there with the rings!" said Alfie, obviously proud of himself. "Even though we're already married, we'd just redo all that, for the pictures. Like Maggie and Dave are doing! Because do-overs are adorbs."

"Those will make for gorgeous photos of our little family," said Wes. "Yes, *adorbs*."

And they walked out to the porch, where their handsome, gracious hosts awaited and a gorgeous sunset was only beginning.

"Well hello, you two!" said Ron, greeting Wes and Alfie as they entered the porch.

"Welcome to the best sunset view in the entire universe," said Dale. "Come sit and have a cocktail with us and enjoy it."

"It's so gorgeous," said Alfie, "we are just so happy to be here."

"You know, we had something really spur of the moment that we wanted to ask you," said Wes. "It's just an idea, but we were thinking, it's so beautiful down here, and of course we don't want to do anything to take away from Dave and Maggie, but what do you think about doing a vow renewal for us?"

"Well, I think your timing is perfect," said Dale. "I was just sitting here with my minister's book reviewing the ceremony options for them. Since they're down here for the shower we were going to be going over them."

"Oh, that's great," said Alfie.

"So how involved is it?" asked Wes.

"Well, it isn't," said Ron. "I mean it depends on what you want. If you want to do a huge ceremony and reception and two hundred people, we can certainly let you do that, and we do it all the time — it's spectacular!"

"But the vow renewal itself is a personal thing between the two of you," said Dale. "As a minister I could perform it right now. You could stand before one another and this gorgeous sunset and you'd be done."

"I love that idea," said Wes. "And that's what we talked about. A private vow renewal."

"And then a very public huge reception later!" said Alfie.

"Yes, with tuxes and music and wine and guests and food," said Wes.

"That, we can definitely help you with!" said Ron.

"We could do it on New Year's Eve for our anniversary," said Wes.

"What a great night for a party!" said Alfie. "Everyone would have such a blast! Fireworks at midnight, champagne, the works!"

"Sounds perfect," said Wes.

Dale paged through his minister's book.

"I have done over two hundred same-sex weddings here at the inn," he said. "And I've put together a brief ceremony that's been very popular for a vow renewal like the one I think you have in mind. It's only about ten minutes long or so. Would you like to try that one?"

"YES!" said Wes and Alfie together.

"Let's do this," said Wes. "I love the spontaneity of the whole thing. Just the two of us and the sunset!"

"OK, here we go!" said Ron. "I love how cozy this is."

Dale began:

"Wes and Alfie, thank you for allowing Ron and I to witness your dedication to one another as you recommit to your union. You have honored us with your friendship and trust today. I pray that your love together may grow stronger and more true in the many days and years ahead of your shared life with one another.

"As you move forward and renew your wedding vows to each other, I ask you to remember that with great happiness can also come great sorrow over time. In relationships we become our true selves, and we do not possess each other. We need solitude as well as togetherness. We are reminded of this by Albert Camus, who said, 'Don't walk before me, I may not follow. Don't walk behind me, I may not lead. Just walk beside me and be my friend.'"

Wes and Alfie looked at one another and smiled, for these words rang true. Ron smiled at Dale. He loved to hear him recite ceremonies—his strong, powerful voice resonated on the large porch with its white columns, high ceilings, and potted ferns blowing in the summer breeze. He knew the reading that was to come, so he stepped out to the kitchen to bring a bottle of champagne and four glasses, that there may be a toast after the brief ceremony.

Dale continued.

"'When you love someone you do not love them all the time, in exactly the same way, from moment to moment. It is an impossibility. It is even a lie to pretend to. And yet this is exactly what most of us demand. We have so little faith in the ebb and flow of life, of love, of relationships. We leap at the flow of the tide and resist in terror its ebb. We are afraid it will never return. We insist on permanency, on duration, on continuity; when the only continuity possible, in life as in love, is in growth, in fluidity—in freedom, in the sense that the dancers are free, barely touching as they pass, but partners in the same pattern. The only real security is not in wanting or possessing, not in demanding or expecting, not in hoping, even. Security in a relationship lies neither in looking to what it was in nostalgia, nor forward to what it might be in dread or anticipation, but living in the present relationship and accepting it as it is now. For relationships, too, must be like islands. One must accept their limits—islands, surrounded by and interrupted by the sea, continually visited and abandoned by the tides. One must accept the security of the winged life, of ebb and flow, of intermittency.'

"I use this quote about islands from Rabindranath Tagore because I feel like a sense of place is so important—that you remember where you were when you renewed your vows, and that you remember this moment together," said Dale. "Please face each other and take each other's hands so that you may see the gift that they are to you.

"These are the hands of your best friend, strong and full of love for you, that are holding yours on the day of the renewal of your wedding vows, as you promise to love each other today, tomorrow, and forever," said Dale. "These are the hands that love you with passion and cherish you wholeheartedly through the years, and with the only a mere touch will be able to comfort you like no other. These are the hands that will provide strength for you when you need it, encouragement and support to pursue your hopes and dreams, and to offer you comfort in difficult times. And finally, these are the hands that many years from now will still reach out for yours, still seeking and providing the same unspoken tenderness with just one touch. "And so, Wes and Alfie, I am going to read a few lines, and then I would like to ask you to read the lines to one another," said Dale. "All right?"

Wes and Alfie, still holding each other's hands so tightly, overwhelmed from the emotion of the previous words, nodded their heads in agreement.

"I come here today to restate my vow to join your life for the rest of my years," said Dale, and Wes and Alfie repeated that line, along with the following lines:

"I pledge to be true to you, to respect you,

and to grow with you throughout these years.

We are so many wonderful things to each other,

May only those best qualities continue to shine

And may our bond continue to grow stronger.

Time will pass, fortune may smile, trials may come;

no matter what we shall encounter together,

I vow here today that our love will be my only love.

I will make my home in your heart from this day until forever."

As Wes and Alfie finished repeating the lines of the vows, Dale cheerfully declared, "I now re-pronounce you husband and husband! You may kiss the groom!"

Wes and Alfie embraced one another, enjoying a long, passionate kiss. The *POP!* of the champagne cork split the air as Ron opened the bottle, pouring four glasses. The men toasted.

"Cheers to the happy couple!" said Ron.

"Here's to many years of wedded bliss," said Dale.

"We can't thank you both enough for this lovely experience," said Wes. "We'll never forget it."

"Oh, it's absolutely been perfect," said Alfie. "You know, somebody should at least get a phone out and get a sunset photo of us with our champagne and this sunset!"

"Gotcha covered," said Ron. "We can't let this moment happen without some documentation."

"You are just so lucky to live here at this gorgeous spot,"

said Wes. "It's a vacation spot for us, and for many people, but for you it's your home!"

"It's the end of the earth," said Ron.

"A little bit of heaven on earth," added Dale.

Chapter 9

"This sunset over the water is the most vibrant, colorful thing I have ever seen," said Lisa, looking out at the Chesapeake Bay from the screened porch.

"When a storm is coming in, the colors are really amazing," said Eva. "The mix of all the reds and oranges at the horizon with the grays and purples in the sky—it makes me wish I had any artistic talent at all, to be able to paint it."

Maggie walked in through the screen door, which thwapped closed behind her. The Black Walnut cabin at Sharps Island Inn, where Lisa and Ben were staying for the weekend, featured a screened porch with a view of the entire southernmost tip of Matthew's Island. Maggie's reddish curls were unrulier than usual from the wind. She held her camera in her hand. Dave, Ben, and Nathan were currently down at Harrison's eating crabs and having a beer—a bachelor party, of sorts.

"These photos are going to be fantastic!" she declared. "I

couldn't stop taking them. All these hammocks—and the way the sun reflects and dances on the water!"

"And they'll remind you of your bridal shower and Eva's baby shower, too," said Lisa.

"Yes, I will frame one for you," said Maggie. "The place is fantastic—isn't it nice we are all here for our wedding shower–baby shower weekend!"

"Thanks, Mags," said Eva. "I really still can't get my head around the fact that a few weeks ago I watched my one-time twin baby boys walk across a graduation stage, and now I'm *having* a baby. It seems surreal."

"Well, if I am not mistaken," said Maggie, "you were just damn thrilled they walked across it at all!"

"True story," said Eva. "You wouldn't believe the crap their father, Joe, and I had to go through with Ken Tracy at the high school to make that magic happen for our little lacrosse-team party boys. Summer classes, tutoring, the works. I also made them go to counseling for the drinking. After my dad's drinking killed him, I don't want to see them self-destruct before they even reach adulthood. The caps and gowns and diplomas in those photos last month were a pure miracle."

"Listen, I know it had to be sad losing your mom not so long ago that she couldn't be there for that, Eva, and with the baby coming... that she won't be here for that too—I've been thinking of you," said Maggie. "But we are here for you."

"Thanks, Maggie," said Eva. "That means a lot."

"You know we are," said Lisa, and she walked into the

kitchen to grab the plate of cheese and crackers she'd made, and a bottle of wine, placing them on the screened porch table. Maggie poured glasses of wine for Lisa and herself, and Lisa brought Eva a glass of ice water.

"What are the boys doing in the fall?" Maggie asked.

"They're staying right here on the Shore where I can watch them," said Eva. "A year at Chesapeake Community College will be good for them, two if they need it, and then if they want to prove that they are ready to go away to college, that will be fine."

"I'm sure they will do well," said Lisa. "They have you for a mom! And you will be so close to them here on the shore. How is everything with your watermen lawsuit?"

"I had a lucky break in the case," said Eva. "There is one judge in Baltimore County who is finally listening to me and isn't in the state's pocket. That's been the real problem up until now. It's all one big circle-jerk; the court system and the state are in bed together and nothing gets done. I basically had to go shopping all around Maryland until I could find a court that would hear the case and make a fair ruling. I think this judge will. She's been around long enough to know all the players, but her family goes back in the watermen's industry for four generations, too, so she's not going to be bullied around by DNR. I've met with the fisheries union and the locals and everyone seems to be on board that maybe we can make it work this time and do some real good here."

"That's so great, Eva," said Lisa. "Nathan must be really

proud."

"Yeah, he's gotta be," added Maggie. "You've worked really hard on this whole thing for a very long time now and put your whole heart and soul into it."

"I have," said Eva. "It wasn't easy making the transition from a full-time court attorney to 'lady of the island' so having something to work on that is meaningful has made all the difference for me. I don't know what I would've done if I didn't have this to work on; I think I would have been a bit stir-crazy."

"Well, he and the rest of those watermen are lucky to have you," said Maggie. "How has he been about the pregnancy and everything?"

"Nathan is so wonderful," said Eva, smiling at Maggie and Lisa, rocking gently in her vintage wooden rocking chair. The breeze was getting slightly stronger as the storm drew closer, but the panoramic view the women had of the sun setting over the Chesapeake was breathtaking. "He is going to be the best father to this baby." She twisted the red sea glass and diamond ring on her finger.

Lisa noticed the ring. "What is *that*?" she asked.

"Oh my God, kiddo. What *is* that, indeed!" Maggie chimed in.

"It's just a ring Nathan gave me," said Eva, beaming. "Made from a piece of sea glass I found here on the island. Isn't it pretty?"

"Gorgeous!" said Lisa. "I've never seen a ring made from

sea glass before. Wow!"

"Stunning," said Maggie. "And perfect for you. It's a piece you found on the beach around here somewhere I'm guessing? So custom made and extra personal. And those look like *diamonds*."

"Yes," said Eva, smiling coyly.

Maggie looked at Lisa. There were a few questions no one had wanted to ask Eva. But if anyone was going to ask them, it would be Maggie.

"So, if you don't mind my asking..." began Maggie.

Eva laughed.

"Oh, Christ, go ahead, Maggie," said Eva. "We are the founding members of the Scarlet Letter Society! We have gone where no women dared tread, or whatever it said on all those invites you used to send. Fire away. There are no secrets here."

"That ring isn't a— er—Do you know... that is, does Nathan know...?" Maggie stammered a bit.

Eva laughed again. "You don't really even know what you're asking me, do you? So many questions, all running together in that curious head of yours. Let me help you. It's not an engagement ring, it's a... well, it was just a very lovely gift, that's all. Nathan knows about the existence of Charles in my past. He does not know that there is a *very* slight chance that Charles could be the father. I have tried a number of times to begin that conversation, but I just haven't had the heart to tell Nathan of that remote possibility. I bought one of those kits, those who's-the-father DNA kits I didn't even know existed, on Amazon.com, and there is a way for me to determine the paternity without Nathan even knowing that I've done it. I've contacted Charles in New York so that I can rule out whether he is the father. I really am quite certain Nathan is the father. In any case, I don't have any remaining feelings for Charles and Nathan is going to be the one raising this baby so I don't want to hurt him…"

There was a moment of awkward silence after Eva's rushed, awkward speech. She sat back in her rocking chair, out of breath, looking a bit exasperated, her cheeks flushed with color.

"What did Charles have to say about that request for… information?" asked Maggie.

"I haven't heard from him yet," said Eva. "I would have gone to New York to talk to him about it in person, but I didn't even know these DNA kits existed until—well, I thought it would be too emotional for me to show up in front him while…"

She motioned to her burgeoning belly.

"That makes perfect sense. What a scene that would have been! Are you and Nathan going to be moving in together?" asked Maggie. "If you don't mind my asking."

"He built the nursery," said Eva. "It's so beautiful. A handmade cradle and everything. He's with me every day and he sleeps at my house every night. We have talked about him selling his house, yes. He really barely goes there anymore. It's almost just a big closet now, so it seems silly to keep it. I think he just didn't want me to feel any pressure to be committed…"

"But having the baby…" said Maggie.

"I know," said Eva. "*There's* a commitment for you, right? But he knew that with the divorce and everything, and now with having a baby, it wasn't like I was going to want to be rushing down the aisle. So talking about formal living arrangements just seemed like one more major life change we didn't need to deal with on top of the baby coming. He knows I like my space. We even talked about building a new house together after everything is more settled down. I think I'd like that."

"I love that he respects your space," said Lisa, sipping her wine and then pulling her blond hair into a ponytail. "Maybe that was the idea with the ring. Just to give you something so beautiful and meaningful, but not so obvious and pressuring as an engagement ring. Something that was a clear symbol of love and commitment, but not something that would make you feel rushed or forced into something like planning a wedding in a certain timeframe while you already had the baby's birth to contend with. It really was beautifully thoughtful in that way."

"Wow, thank you, Lisa, that's a really lovely way to put it. So what about your love life, lady baker?" asked Eva. "Enough about me, geez! How's everything with your happy little home?"

"Oh, gosh, Eva, everything's really great," said Lisa. "Ben makes me so happy and I love living in town. It's nice having the weekend off from the bakery. I hope you ladies like the cakes I made for the shower tomorrow!"

"We like everything you make," said Maggie. "So how's Max?"

"He is just the best little guy," said Lisa. "He invited me to his class for career day to talk about being a baker and they let me bring treats for the kids so I made these colorful chocolate-covered pretzels and they were really a hit."

"Oh yeah," said Eva. "My boys never wanted me to come for that. Who wants a boring corporate attorney at career day? But chocolate-covered pretzels? That's a winner right there."

"It was a little odd because I knew some of the other parents who were there knew I wasn't his mom," said Lisa. "I mean no one asked me about it. But you could tell..."

"Yeah, well, I bet some of the other parents also know his mom sorta skipped town so she isn't exactly going to be showing up for career day anytime soon," said Maggie. "And they're not gonna say anything to your face about it. Of course they had to make you feel like shit though. These bitches prefer to talk about people behind their backs. Fucking Queefalopes."

"Oh geez, here we go," said Eva.

"Queefa-*lope*?" asked Lisa, genuinely mystified. "What is that?"

"Even *I* don't know that one," said Eva. "Thundercunt and

Cuntasaurus Rex have been covered in previous editions of the 'Maggie's Massive Insult Dictionary,' but this one doesn't even have the 'c' word in it, so please enlighten us."

"Oh, come on, you guys, I don't make these words up, they're real, I'm sure you can look them up on the Internet," said Maggie. "We used to call people queefs all the time in high school in the eighties. You know what that is, right? It's cunt fart, like that noise you make during sex?"

"OK, *that* is familiar now," said Eva. "Haven't heard that one in a while. Real trip down memory lane there, Maggie. Ever charming!"

"Yeah, well, a Queefalope is like the female queef animal — just some bitch who won't say something to your face, like these idiot moms at Max's school," said Maggie. "So who gives a shit about them, Lisa. Max loves you, and Ben loves you, and that's all that matters."

"Agreed!" said Lisa. "If I see them again maybe I can sneeze loudly and say 'Queefalope' under my breath and then try not to start laughing!"

"There ya go," said Maggie.

"Thanks for that! Isn't this sunset stunning?" said Lisa. "But it's unbelievable how quickly the weather changes around here."

The women watched as the storm rolled in. The gray clouds crushed the orange at the horizon line. The winds whipped the bay toward the rocky shoreline, causing waves to splash up and onto the lawn. In the distance, thunder rolled and far across the Talbot River, the first lightning strikes began.

"The sunsets are pretty," said Eva, "but I love the storms on the island just as much. There is something so powerful about their energy. When the storms come, everything else stops. They're in charge."

"Wow, that's actually pretty cool," said Maggie. "I like the fickle weather. I want to stay right here on this porch until it starts raining so hard that it's blowing in on us. I love watching this sky. So, I have something pretty odd to share with you ladies."

"What is it?" asked Eva.

"I got a letter from my mother," said Maggie.

"Your mother?" said Lisa. "I know you've only mentioned her once or twice, ever…"

"Oh my God," said Eva, "so she's alive?"

"Yeah, well there's a reason I haven't mentioned her, Lisa," said Maggie, "which is that she abandoned me when I was six years old. I didn't even know her goddamn name until I got this letter. Couldn't have even told you she was still alive, Eva."

"Jesus, Maggie," said Eva. "I don't even know what to say."

"Well, there isn't much to say," said Maggie. "I've been trying to decide what to do about it. I brought the letter down here to read to you girls and see what you think about it. You ready?"

Lisa and Eva nodded their heads as Maggie began to read.

Dear Maggie,

    I know it is really shocking to get a letter from me now after all these years have past. My name is Susan and I am your mother. I'm 65 years old, and I am dying from ovarian cancer. I am writing this letter because I want to apologize to you for leaving you.

    I had you when I was 15 years old. You were named for my Irish grandmother Margaret who I loved so much. My family was really poor and Catholic in Boston and I had hid my pregnancy from them. My oldest sister let me live with her for some time but then she had another child and so there wasn't any more room. I tried to live on my own with you for a long time but I couldn't pay the rent or heat anymore. I loved you so much and did the best I knew to take care of you when I worked waitressing at night.

    I worried every shift I worked at that something would happen to you and I couldn't pay a sitter. I couldn't let you keep being cold anymore. A woman from my work told me if I let you stay in foster care, that I would be able to visit you, but they only let me come one time and then that family you were with moved away, and I didn't even know where. I was 23 and didn't have any money. I went to the office and wrote letters (there wasn't any Internet then) but the foster system wouldn't tell me where you moved to no matter what I did.

It took me a lot of years, and finally, until this age of my life and hiring private investigators, to find you. I later got married, but I never had another child. The thought of when I lost you was way too painful for me to ever even think about having another baby. My husband had a heart attack 7 years ago and died. I saved his life insurance money from the fire company for my retirement but I won't be needing that now so I used part of it to find you.

I understand if you do not want to have anything to do with me. But I want you to know that I love you, I have always loved you, and that I am sorry. The investigators told me that you have two older daughters, and I can't believe it but they are my granddaughters. If there is somehow a way you would consider visiting me, I would be so thankful. I am sorry to put all this on you. I just wanted you to know you were never forgotten.

I hope you can forgive me.

Sending you my love,
Your mother,
Susan

Maggie looked up from the letter and as soon as she lifted her face, the tears ran down her cheeks. Lisa immediately stood—it took Eva a moment longer in her third trimester of pregnancy to rise—and they walked over to Maggie's rocking chair. Maggie stood, and the three friends embraced.

The rain had started to blow in. Maggie returned the letter to her back pocket, and the women gathered their snacks and drinks and went inside. There was a gas fireplace, and a cozy sofa where they could enjoy front-row seats to a picture-window view of the storm over the river, and to their right, the porch view over the bay: a surround-sound IMAX storm.

"I know you said you wanted to ask us about what to do," said Eva. "But that is such a hugely personal choice. That had to be a shock when that showed up—bringing up such a major part of your past. I can't even imagine how you must be feeling. When did you get the letter?"

"It just came the day before yesterday to my shop," said Maggie. "I guess her 'investigator' must have found my address there in Keytown? Anyway I figured I'd just bring it down here and share it with you guys in person. I've been in tears off and on since I got it. And you both know I am not a big crier."

"What have Dave and your girls said?" asked Lisa.

"It's just such a shock to all of us," said Maggie. "Obviously they support whatever I wanna do, I mean, throw it out, go see her, whatever. I don't know how sick she is. Dying can be tomorrow or she just got diagnosed, I don't know."

"Did she leave a phone number?" asked Eva.

"No, it's weird, she didn't," said Maggie. "We can just look it up though. I'm not just going to show up on her doorstep. She asks in the letter for me to visit her, but doesn't say anything about calling. But Dave looked up the address and it's a nursing care facility of some sort, so she must be pretty bad off."

"Oh, wow," said Lisa. "That had to be pretty shocking."

"Yeah, I guess you have no way of knowing what kind of shape she is in, if that affects your decision either way," said Eva. "I suppose you could call the facility and speak with a nurse and explain the situation and they might tell you what her physical condition is. And then, in theory, if there were visiting hours…"

"Yeah, well, I'm not ready to hop on a plane to Boston and show up with flowers in my hand after more than forty years and pop in like, 'Hey, Mom! What's new?'" said Maggie, as she sipped from her merlot. She ran a hand through her unruly mop of red curls, her face reddening. "I'm just gonna need to give it some thought for a little bit."

"That is totally understandable," said Lisa, sensing Maggie didn't want to talk about the letter anymore. "My family is a mess. It's why I never talk about them. I hadn't seen my parents or my sister in years when my dad died of cancer. My entire childhood was spent taking care of my brother Tommy, who was in a wheelchair and severely mentally disabled. My parents always worked full time. A nurse came to the house part time for my brother's medical needs, but no one ever talked to him, not even my sister, no one but me. It was like I was the only one who acknowledged he was even a person. When I left after high school for culinary school in DC, they took him to a full-time residential facility there. I had to go and be the one to tell my brother when Dad died, and he seemed upset but I don't even really know, it's hard to say whether he understood what I meant. I think he did. I did go to my father's funeral, and I was sorry to see my mother and my sister so upset. But that was the last time I saw them, ten years ago. I still visit my brother once a week."

"Lisa, you never talk about your brother," said Eva. "Or any of them."

"I know," said Lisa. "It's just that talking about him makes me think of how much I hate being so distanced from my family even though it's for a reason. It's why you didn't hear me talk about my mother or my sister when Jim died, too. Dysfunctional family stuff just is what it is, and we can't really change it and to me, talking about it just doesn't really help anything."

"I'm glad you shared it with us though," said Maggie. "It sounds like you had a lot on your plate growing up."

"Yeah, Lisa, I am really sorry you had to go through all that too. Well, since it's the dysfunction junction hour, I'll be really honest about something," said Eva. "I had a sister too."

"What?" said Maggie. "I have always thought you were an only child!"

"I've always said that," said Eva. "But growing up I had a little sister, Janie. We used to hide in the closet together when Dad would be so drunk that he would hit Mom. It was so terrifying to be a child and be inside that closet. We would just run into the nearest closet, and this one night we were in the tiny living room closet together and Dad had come home from work drunk and he was just screaming at Mom about dinner not being ready or something stupid like that. I was about four and Janie was maybe two and a half. And he was hitting Mom right outside the closet door and Janie just said to me '*Help Mommy*' and she ran out of the closet before I could stop her..."

Eva paused, taking in a deep breath.

"Man, I would do anything for a glass of wine right now," said Eva. She fought back tears, continuing, "... She threw open the closet door, and it was so loud, the way it slammed the wall, and that asshole was right there and I don't know whether it just scared him, that door slamming open like that, whether he meant to hurt her or he was just too drunk, but he slapped her backward and her head hit the trim on the door frame and she fell to the floor and she was unconscious. Mom screamed and I can still hear that scream today in my head. Mom picked us both up and ran out the door and she took me to the next door neighbor's house in my pajamas. She took Janie to the hospital but Janie never came home. I didn't go to her funeral because there wasn't one and I was too little to know why but now I know. It's because my drunk asshole of a father didn't want anyone to know that he had killed his own daughter. And even worse than that, my mother didn't want anyone to know that she was too much of a coward to have called the cops. He swore to my mother that he would kill me if she called the cops. They just kept telling people that she fell. That's how I got to be an only child."

"Oh, Eva," said Lisa. "I can't even comprehend having to live with those images in your head your whole life. I'm so sorry."

"Holy shit, Eva, you never told me," said Maggie. "But I can understand why. Those are some nasty demons. I'm really sorry, kid. Man, what a mess we all turned out to be, friends. But you know what? There aren't any normal families anywhere but on TV."

Eva wiped away her tears.

"You're right. You know, it feels good to get that story out of my system," said Eva. "I carried that around for a long time. Never been to therapy or anything like that. I was really worried I was drinking too much. I have Charles to thank for that actually. I didn't want to end up like my dad. Walking on the beach on this island since my mother died, finding the peace that comes with sea glass hunting, I thought about it and realized I needed to get a little help, so I went to a few AA meetings at the church."

"You did?" asked Maggie. "I have to say, Eva, I never thought of you as an alcoholic. I know you like your wine."

"I don't know about labels," said Eva, "but I want to be

healthy. I don't want those demons, as you call them, and that's just what they are—I don't want those haunting me with the future of the new baby I have on the way. I feel guilty about the boys, like they deserved a better mom. I feel like maybe I am getting a second chance."

"That sweet baby," said Maggie. "So happy for you. It's not true about the boys. They love you."

"You know they do, Eva. And they graduated from high school, so you must have done something right! Have you picked out any baby names yet?" asked Lisa. "Or have you and Nathan found out if it's a boy or girl?"

"No none of that," said Eva. "Just hoping for an easy delivery and a healthy baby."

"I hope that for you too," said Maggie. "Looks like the boys are pulling up the driveway—hope they had a nice crab feast!"

"I'm sure they did, even though they may have had to move inside to eat some of them!" said Eva. "You can't go wrong with crabs on a summer night on the island."

"I saw the weather forecast is nicer for tomorrow night and the baby/bridal shower and fireworks!" said Lisa.

"That's great," said Maggie. "We can all get in the pool and watch the show. I'd love to get a photo of the fireworks reflecting over the bay. This place is going to be gorgeous for my wedding on Labor Day weekend—I already can't wait to come back!"

"That's one we will all want to frame," said Eva. "Thanks

for listening, friends. And Maggie, let us know what you decide about your mother."

"I feel lucky to have friends like you," said Lisa.

"I will let you know," said Maggie, looking at Eva. She turned to Lisa. "And I feel lucky too.

"We all shared a lot tonight," Maggie said then. "There was an old quote I heard once. Something about 'she never knew the weight until she felt the freedom.' Seems about right. So until tomorrow! We might not have close sisters in our families, but we have chosen each other as sisters. We could change our name: *The Scarlet Letter Sisters*."

"Goodnight, sisters," said Eva.

"Goodnight, sisters," said Lisa.

"Goodnight, my sisters," said Maggie.

THE NEXT day, Maggie and Eva would unwrap lovely bridal and baby shower gifts, and their friends and guests would enjoy the music and delicious cake, all pleased to celebrate the happy life events. But the sunset chat between the three best friends, such rare moments when women could spend time amongst one another sharing hopes and dreams and loss and support, without husbands or jobs or kids demanding their attention, it was this precious time at Sharps Island Inn that the women would treasure for years to come.

Chapter 10

The wind howled outside in the raging late summer storm, causing the candles that lit the dungeon to flicker. Jo and Kevin were filming a scene, but they didn't want to be identified as the actors, so Kevin was wearing a medieval-style leather hood with a steel grid across the mouth for breathing. He was currently lying face-up on the wooden bondage table above a built-in steel cage, affixed at several points by his wrists and ankles.

Jo was wearing a blond wig featuring bangs and a neat, angled shoulder-length haircut. Her false eyelashes and heavy black and purple makeup made her nearly unrecognizable as her normal self. She was a completely different character. Zarina had seen her from the control room on the video screen when she hung up the phone, but still barely knew it was her when she went rushing downstairs and into the room, something she would normally never do.

After making an announcement through the control room

speaker ("PAUSE FILMING!"), Zarina knocked loudly on the door, calling on her way down the steps per the custom in such a set of extenuating circumstances.

"PAUSE FILMING!" Zarina had cried again, panting. It was a phrase reserved for when the authorities were suspected, or someone's spouse showed up on the premises; literally instances that occurred twice in the entire time they'd been there, under those two exact circumstances.

Jo calmly turned from the wooden cabinet on the wall in the corner of the room where she had been selecting a flogger. She wore a purple leather bustier that forced her D-size breasts to heave over the top of the structured cone-shape, black lace rimmed top. Shiny purple leather booty shorts, purple leather gloves, and black fishnet stockings completed the shiny, dramatic outfit. She cocked her head slightly, examining Zarina curiously. Jo took three steps toward her on four-inch patent leather purple platform heels. Zarina tried not to stare at her. She heard "None of Your Business" by Salt-N-Pepa begin playing on the sound system, and cursed herself for not having turned it off.

"Pardon me?" said Jo, who had chosen a tool from the vast selection.

When Jo was in the dungeon, she was not a business owner at VXD Enterprises and she was definitely not a schoolteacher at Matthew's Island Elementary School. She was a prima domme dominatrix of the highest order, the queen of her world and certainly the world of those around her. Her submissives, both in this room and the tens of thousands of followers she had online, worshipped her, went onto their knees for her, followed her every command, waiting without breathing for her next tiny move. She was in full and total control and she certainly did not take an order from another human being under any circumstances. She spent between one and two hours getting into her makeup and costuming for this role—this *world*—and during that time a mental and psychological transformation took place as well. It wasn't just a character, like in a movie, it was a lifestyle, an embodiment of an entire psyche—it was *who she was*.

From behind thick black eyelashes, Jo blinked slowly at Zarina, like a very confident cat would blink at a mouse who had come into its space, knowing the mouse had absolutely no way of escaping the same way it had entered.

"And she wanna be a freak and sell it on the weekend..."

Zarina listened to the music, because it helped her concentrate on something and calm her nerves. It was better than listening to the thunder and lightning. She stole a glance over at Kevin. His breath quickened on the dungeon table. The entry of another woman into the space was obviously arousing. Zarina assumed that underneath that crazy-looking leather hood, he still knew it was her, since no one else would dare enter the space.

Jo saw her looking at Kevin, and did not have to look over to imagine exactly what *he* was thinking—it was a game she liked to play, and she knew she was good at it:

Exotic, innocent Zarina, with her flawless caramel-colored skin and long black hair and those bright, intelligent eyes — he tried not to think of how young and hot she was, he'd always had a crush on her — because he was lying there naked and if Jo saw him get excited, she would punish him for hours on end. His wrist and ankle handcuffs clinked ever slightly as he ironically strained to stay calm, trying to use breathing methods practiced over time.

Jo noticed everything, always, and she didn't have to imagine the clinking of Kevin's restlessness, the change in his breath pattern, because she heard those smaller sounds, even with the storm outside. She knew if she turned her head, she'd see the twitching in his cock as it pulsed slightly.

"Hello, Zarina," said Jo.

Zarina swallowed. *Said the spider to the fly* went immediately through her mind. Which was ridiculous! This was her business partner! Why would she be afraid of her? She simply had to tell her what happened that caused her to run downstairs without any notice. She tried not to look around the dungeon. It looked so much bigger down here than on the screen, which was how she was used to seeing it. This was the longest she'd ever been down here — the other two times involved the first two emergency notifications: the police raid had turned out to be nothing (some DNR guy thought seafood was still being run out of the warehouse) and the spouse visit was deflected without the spouse coming down to the space, though a marriage may have ended when the woman saw her husband with four leather-clad actors, including men.

Zarina swallowed, trying to keep the nervousness that didn't belong there in the first place out of her voice. "I'm really sorry for interrupting," began Zarina. "It's just that something came up that I thought you really needed to know about right away…"

Zarina wasn't sure where to look, but she definitely tried not to look again at Kevin. Her eyes stayed focused on Jo, on the candy-apple-red glistening lipstick of her pursed lips, smiling at the corners. Even looking at Jo wasn't easy, she was so… *evocative*. She thought back to the time Jo had barely brushed her arm in the studio and felt a tingling in the center of her body. The dungeon was drafty, which added to the effect. Zarina was wearing a cotton tank top and a cotton-spandex skirt, and she wrapped her arms around herself, perhaps to protect herself from the cold, but also somehow from Jo's intent gaze, and impossibly, from the wind that rattled the old windows. The island was in the middle of yet another storm — they seemed to hit constantly nowadays. From down here below the main floor of the warehouse, Zarina could hear a few leaks in the ancient building; the distant drip-drip-dripping of the downpour, echoes in the darkness in a few places that seemed to accent the surroundings perfectly and weren't something she could see in a video up in the control room.

"Well, go on," said Jo, "what's the emergency?"

As she spoke, she walked closer to Zarina. In her hand was a lavender swivel-head deerskin suede flogger with twenty-four lashes she'd chosen from the cabinet. She gently swung it around on its hinge.

With the nature of her business and her personality, Jo was a bit of a flogger connoisseur. She had two dozen, ranging in sizes and shapes and materials. The construction and the number of the strands of leather determined whether there was more of a sting or a thudding sensation; each felt entirely different when used on her clients. The way the leather was wrapped around the hilt of the handle and how it felt in her hand as she used it were also important—this swivel-head design protected Jo's wrist from overuse; it was one of her favorites, and as she clicked past Zarina in the purple platform heels on the ancient hardwood floor, she grazed the tendrils of suede gently across the back sides of Zarina's knees.

Zarina did everything in her power to remain standing. The sensation of the soft suede was mesmerizing—she thought of the dungeon as a place filled with whips and chains and pain, and the feeling she was experiencing was the opposite. The tingle from the backs of her knees, like the time Jo touched her arm, was electrified and it traveled through the nerve endings inside her, along deep channels within and around her brain, touching every sexual fiber. *What the hell is happening to me?* thought Zarina. She struggled to stay focused.

"It's your boss," said Zarina, rushing the words out. "The principal of the elementary school. Mr. Spannek. He called here. On the business line. He asked to speak to you. I just thought that was very shocking and I thought you'd want to know about it right away."

She exhaled, pleased to have finally gotten all the words out.

Jo broke out into a hysterical, near-cackling laughter. The sound bounced around the large steel panels that had been hung from the walls and ceiling for effect as background in the videos. "Principal Dickhead called here on the landline phone?" She laughed again. "Well, that's a new one. What the fuck does he want?"

"He didn't say. What does he know about our — video production company?" asked Zarina.

"Who cares?" said Jo. "I'll have to ask him in the faculty meeting tomorrow. But for now, I'm far more interested in the fact that you are standing here, finally, after all this time, in *my space*. I know you've been wanting to come down here. You know I've been wanting you to come down here. And you are looking very curious about what Kevin and I have going on here in my dungeon."

"I'm really sorry to have interrupted..." Zarina stammered for words.

Jo smiled at the apology. Her unintentional submission was a step in the right direction.

"Would you like to stay and play?" asked Jo. "I could show you the ropes."

Jo smiled at her. Zarina heard the first strains of "Give Me Tonight" by Shannon start on the sound system, and she smiled back at her, for one moment recognizing her friend and business partner underneath the makeup and wig and purple leather get-up, and the tension was eased. But in that same moment, Zarina felt the magnetic pull of her attraction to Jo more strongly than she ever had before. They had flirted casually before, but this experience was on a totally different level, and Zarina knew there was no going back. She also knew the cameras were running, and that her husband, Stanley, would be so massively turned on by this footage that he'd thank her forever. She decided to just relax and enjoy. Why not play along and have some fun? This wasn't the first time Zarina had been with a girl, or even in a threesome, and Stanley knew that. Lucky for her, he was very liberal about the whole thing.

"I would love to stay and play, Mistress Jo," said Zarina. "But I'm very new at this and don't know any of the rules of the game."

"Oh, you know I like to teach," said Jo. "You've already met my student Kevin."

Zarina watched as Jo walked over to the bondage table where Kevin was splayed, naked, only able to listen to the exchange so far. Now, Jo removed the leather hood so he could see the women.

"Greet Zarina, Kevin," said Jo. She slapped him lightly on the thigh with her purple leather glove.

"Hello, Zarina," said Kevin.

"Hi, Kevin," said Zarina, which seemed awkward to her because they'd known each other for years. Of course, she'd never seen him naked and handcuffed to a leather bondage table with a built-in cage below it before, his ankles cuffed to the metal loops at the corners of the table. She thought about making a joke about how they'd shake hands under other circumstances, and then thought better of it. She did not think Jo would think it was funny. Jo was clearly in charge of the conversation, and it wasn't the time to joke around.

"Give me tonight... then if you don't wanna stay... girl, I'll just forget you..."

"I don't normally like surprises," said Jo. "But I have to say I'm intrigued by this one today."

Standing beside him, Jo gently dragged the flogger's flails across Kevin's thighs and ever lightly across his cock, which stiffened in response to the strands of soft leather. At the moment, Jo was using the flogger gently while he was on his back; she normally used it with more force when he was lying face-down, his penis jutting through the hole in the table and exposed from the cage side. She could flog his backside this way, occasionally reaching under the table to feel how hard he was.

Jo twisted one of Kevin's nipples and he cried out with a very soft sound.

Zarina watched in awe.

"Come closer, Zarina," said Jo. "I won't hurt you. Yet."

Zarina did as she was told and walked over to the table.

"Does it excite you to see Kevin so aroused?" asked Jo. She slapped Kevin's thigh lightly with the flogger in her right hand, slowly moving it again across his torso, across his throbbing cock.

Zarina's breathing had become more shallow. She looked at Jo. Jo slowly ran her left hand up her torso and slid it inside the top of her purple leather bustier, lifting her right breast until her nipple was exposed. Zarina and Kevin both watched Jo as she tightly twisted and turned her nipple between her fingers, her own breathing becoming heavier.

"Yes," said Zarina. "It's very exciting." She didn't know what to do with her hands, her eyes... but she did know one thing: Jo was in charge.

Kevin pulled against the restraints; the clanking of the metal loops and the stretching of the leather straps that held the cuffs were the only sounds besides the pelting of the rain against the windows and the sounds of their breathing. The CD had ended upstairs, and the threesome was making their own soundtrack now.

"Why don't you hold this for me?" said Jo, raising the flogger. "See how it feels in your hand."

Jo held out the lavender suede flogger in both her palms, presenting it to Zarina. Kevin took a deep breath, which Jo immediately interpreted as surprise: she knew he was certain no one had ever before held one of her tools.

Zarina tentatively took the foreign object, holding out both her upturned palms to accept it as though she were inside some sort of bizarre video game accepting a sword because she had completed one level and was now going to be headed to the next level. Then she felt odd holding it that way, so she gripped the handle in her right fist, the way it was meant to be held. The twenty-four flails immediately responded as they should on their hinge, pivoting almost automatically. She steadied them with her left hand, surprised at the softness of the suede.

Jo smiled. "See, that's not so scary, is it?"

Zarina looked up and Jo had now removed both her breasts from the top of the bustier. She was using one of her leather gloves to work Kevin's cock and the other glove to pinch and twist her own nipple. She expertly hopped onto the table, straddling Kevin, which revealed the fact that her booty shorts had no center material and therefore her shaved mound was now on prominent display. Letting go of her nipple, she attended herself with two fingers. The scene was very erotic. Zarina would have been happy just to watch, but she had also become extremely excited herself.

"Would you like me to tell you what to do?" said Jo. "Wouldn't it just be so much easier if someone else was in control right now?"

Zarina quickly nodded her head yes. As she stroked herself, Jo gave a brief speech about BDSM, something Zarina had earlier learned was a somewhat confusing acronym that stood for bondage & discipline, dominance & submission, sadism & masochism.

"Normally when we enter dominant-submissive relationships we have signed contracts and we agree to very specific sets of rules that establish our relationship," said Jo, "but if you would like to verbally agree that today is simply for play, I would be willing to agree to enter a simple roleplay session."

"Yes," said Zarina. "Anything you say."

"For starters, that's 'Anything you say, *Empress Josephine,'*" said Jo, still working Kevin's dick slowly while she slowly stroked herself. "When you speak to me in this space, you shall refer to me as 'Empress Josephine' because I reign over any and all activities here."

"Yes, Empress Josephine," said Zarina, wishing she could start touching her own aching center. In her mind as the words echoed, Zarina couldn't help but think they sounded a little bit like the words *impress Josephine,* and it made her a little bit more nervous. She tried to push the thought aside. She wished the dungeon came with strong drinks first.

"Good," said Jo. "Now the first thing we're going to need to do is get you naked and tie you up."

Zarina was past the point of shock at this point, so she just stood motionless, wishing the imaginary drinks had been a double.

Jo climbed down from the table, walked over, took the flogger from Zarina, and placed it next to Kevin on the table.

"We'll be needing you in a little bit, Kevin," said Jo, "but for now you can just watch."

He nodded his head in agreement. No arguments there.

"One of the most enticing elements of the BDSM lifestyle

is the anticipation," said Jo to Zarina. "So one of the things you're going to learn today is that the waiting is just as exciting as the action. Take off your clothes," Jo ordered.

Jo walked over to the large wooden cupboard and removed a few items while Zarina did what she had been told. She was a bit self-conscious to be naked in front of Kevin, but he thoughtfully looked away while she undressed, to give her privacy.

Jo returned slowly, the tap of each heel creating suspense for both Zarina and Kevin. She took note that every goose bump had been raised on Zarina's skin.

She walked over to Zarina, now carrying a small black leather riding crop with a red triangular tip, which she showed to Zarina. The riding crop tucked under her arm, she wrapped a red silk blindfold around Zarina's eyes. She walked over and placed the riding crop next to the flogger.

"Suspense is all part of the game," said Jo. "Not knowing what's coming next."

She then returned to Zarina, put her wrists behind her back, and tied them tightly, expertly with a silk handkerchief. For this play session there was no need for handcuffs or rope that might frighten her. Bondage could be accomplished with materials that felt luxurious.

Once her wrists were tied, Jo picked the riding crop back up. "The item you saw me holding is a riding crop. It has a tapping sensation like this..."

Jo tapped the crop on Zarina's outer thigh. Zarina drew in a breath.

"We think of these tools as being used for pain when really they create far more pleasure," said Jo.

Jo tapped the crop gently, swiftly along Zarina's thigh, up her sides, and around to her ass, occasionally tapping a bit harder, but never painfully. Swiftly, she tapped on her nipples, first one, then the other.

"How does that feel?" asked Jo.

Zarina's breathing was very quick.

"Exciting," she answered.

Jo responded by running one of her leather gloves along Zarina's torso and gently along her ass.

"And this?" she asked.

"Yes," Zarina simply answered.

Jo slapped her harder on her right ass cheek with the riding crop and as Zarina drew in a gasp, she kissed her full on the mouth. Zarina responded by returning the kiss. Jo took Zarina's left nipple into her hand, twisting it with a medium pressure, and Zarina's entire body responded. She was already fully wet from the excitement of the room's sexual tension, even from just seeing Jo in her sexy attire, the full power of her sexuality, but this physical encounter was astronomically arousing.

Jo was surprised herself at how aroused she was by the kiss. Zarina's lips were so soft, her body so inviting, her willingness to learn so complete. The sexual tension between them had been there for years but had remained at a low hum—their business and friendship had come first. Unleashed, though, its power was a force unrelenting and dynamic. Jo had to pull herself back together to remember who was in control.

She walked over to Kevin.

"This has to be fun for you to watch," said Jo. "Something new in the dungeon today, right?"

Kevin smiled. He couldn't help it.

She smiled in return. Seeing he didn't need further arousal, she released his wrists and ankles from the cuffs.

"You've been restrained long enough, Kevin," said Jo, "and besides, we're having a play session and I wouldn't want you to miss out on all the fun."

Kevin remained where he was, awaiting further instruction. But Jo was aroused and she needed satisfaction. She jumped onto the table and grabbed the leather loops that hung above it. Her body was toned from basically using these as pull-up straps, for leverage.

She didn't have to say anything to him. Her hands in the leather straps, her legs splayed at the knees, she simply motioned downward with her eyes at her own body. He moved quickly into a sitting position, taking her nipple into his mouth, using his tongue to arouse her, looking pleased to finally have an opportunity to do so. His hand traveled across her thighs, down her back. He knew that in the rare event she chose to be touched, she liked to have every other part of her skin touched first before he moved to her center.

Kevin wasn't just the head filmmaker, or a typical client for the purposes of web videos, he was also her lover outside the dungeon.

Zarina listened to the sexual sounds, unable to see anything through the blindfold, and wished she could observe what was going on. Were they fucking? She wanted to watch. She wanted to say something, but dared not. She had to wait, just like Jo had said. This was what Kevin must have felt like when he was wearing that leather hood. She couldn't touch herself to soothe the maddening, pulsing ache. She waited.

"Let's not leave Zarina out of the party," said Jo. She climbed down from the bondage table, kissing Kevin, and standing beside the table, she let her tongue drag slowly, lightly down his neck, chest, and across his groin. She paused to take his arousal into her mouth, using her leather glove to work his rock-hard shaft firmly, twisting it while she worked her tongue. He exhaled with pleasure, but she wouldn't let him get anywhere close to orgasm—there was still plenty of work to be done. She released him, motioning her head toward Zarina. He took her lead, getting down from the table and following her.

She picked up the flogger and the riding crop. "We're going to need some more space." Jo walked over and opened a door leading to another room.

The small finished bedroom adjacent to the dungeon was used for filming group scenes. Featuring white walls and a black iron four-post bondage post bed with a red leather mattress, it was appointed with all the equipment for any BDSM fantasy scene. Cameras hung in each corner of the room to capture the action.

She walked back over to Zarina. Riding crop in hand, she tapped it quickly and gently along Zarina's sides and ass to bring her flesh back into a state of awareness. Zarina stood up straight, tossing her silky black hair over one shoulder; her arms restrained from managing it. Jo gathered all her hair into one leather glove.

"Beautiful," she said. She ran her glove down the length of Zarina's hair, twisting it into a ponytail, pulling it slightly tighter. Using the riding crop, she tapped Zarina's nipples.

"My hands are full," she said to Kevin, having tucked the flogger under one arm. "Could you hold this please?" She handed him the crop. Taking the suede flogger, and still holding Zarina's hair tightly with her left hand, she grazed it across Zarina's naked back and down her ass. Standing directly behind her so that Zarina could feel Jo's body touching her from behind, Jo first tightened the handful of hair, hard, then let it go. She wrapped her right arm around Zarina, letting the flogger fall and braise the front of Zarina's body, tapping her inner thighs, abdomen, breasts, and erogenous zones with its twenty-four soft, leathery tendrils. Jo felt Zarina's body soften, as though it was melting against her. Jo let her left hand slide slowly up the side of Zarina's thigh, up the curve of her torso, and around to her left breast, finding soft roundness, the nipple completely hard from excitement. Jo twisted the nipple, with a medium amount of pressure, and Zarina's body jolted with simultaneous surprise, pleasure, excitement. Jo let the flogger fall on Zarina's inner thigh at that moment, not for pain, but for sensation, knowing exactly how to let the suede land so it brought even more sensation.

Kevin watched, and unable to contain his excitement he looked at Jo, resigned to the amount of torture he'd been through already, he was overwhelmed with desire, and she knew instinctively that he was asking for permission. She nodded slightly, and he slowly began to work his own shaft as he watched the women. Obviously happy to be able to move around again, Kevin's left hand swiped his face and ran through his cropped white hair as he rolled his head in a circle, stretching his neck around and taking in the glorious scene with his hazel-green eyes. The former Naval Academy pilot's right hand ran across his muscular chest, a few fingers slid by his rigid nipples, across the ridges on his abdomen, and down to his aching dick. She smiled at his arousal, looking at him sexily and running her tongue across her top lip, knowing it was a fantasy for him to watch this scene.

"We'll be needing your services shortly, Kevin," Jo said as she continued to roll and gently drop the flogger around Zarina's torso, thighs, back, breasts.

Kevin flexed his ass cheek muscles, bit his lower lip, rolled his hips, and narrowed his sexy eyes at her in response, which made Jo wetter than she already was. Using his right grip at the base of his cock, he showed her the full attention of his desire, rolling two fingers from his left hand first across the glistening end of his shaft and then across his left nipple.

He rolled his tongue across his upper lip, narrowing those hazel green eyes at her. Jo closed her eyes, sighing, and had to place two fingers through the slit in her shorts to address her own excruciating need, but for the moment she returned her attention to Zarina. She walked around to the front of Zarina, who was visibly shaking from arousal and suspense.

Then Jo did something she didn't usually do, especially in her own dungeon. Partially in response to Kevin's bold display of arousal, partly in response to her own excitement and Zarina's, she put down the riding crop and got down on her knees facing Zarina. Her gloved hands traveled up Zarina's soft body to her breasts, where she used her fingers to pinch and twist the nipples to full attention in anticipation of her tongue. She grazed one nipple with her teeth, then the other. She sucked each tit until Zarina cried out in pleasure, using her fingers to circle and tease Zarina's clit expertly at the same time. Zarina orgasmed, barely standing, feeling as though she were going to collapse against Jo.

Jo looked at Kevin. He was breathing heavily and had stopped pleasuring himself; Jo knew it was because he was close to orgasm. She stood up. "Let's all move to the bedroom, shall we?" she said.

She removed Zarina's blindfold and wrist restraint. Zarina, panting, blinked at her, wide-eyed, smiling, dazed.

"So you've learned the lesson of what it's like to use your other senses when you don't have sight or touch," said Jo. "Now for the rest of the play session, I'm going to allow you to watch and feel. I wouldn't want you to miss out on the full experience."

"Kevin," said Jo, "Zarina is in a bit of a weakened state. Would you do me a favor and transport our dungeon guest to the bed?"

"Of course, Empress," said Kevin. He walked over, swooped Zarina off her feet, cradling her, and carried her to the red leather mattress of the bondage bed, placing her down gently on her back.

"Jo—" began Zarina, "I feel like I want to... like I should..."

Jo laughed. "Luckily this is a play session," said Jo, "or you would be severely punished right now. First of all for addressing me the wrong way, but mostly for trying to tell me what you want, which is completely insignificant in this space. Here, you are submissive. Your wants are determined by me. And, from what I've seen so far, being met. So how about you just relax and enjoy the ride, OK, Zarina?"

Zarina blushed, nodding.

"Yes, Empress Josephine," she responded.

"Much better," said Jo.

The four-poster bondage bed featured leather straps with heavy steel cuffs. Jo removed matching steel wrist and ankle cuffs from hooks on the wall and attached them to Zarina's wrists and ankles, securing them in place. She was in a comfortable position—her arms and legs had a certain range of movement without being outstretched too far.

Jo walked around to the other side of the bed and started

kissing Kevin. She placed her hands on his muscular, curved ass, squeezing the cheeks hard, while Zarina watched.

"I don't want to neglect you," she said to Kevin, darting a tongue into his mouth. "Did you like watching me with Zarina?"

"Very much, Empress," said Kevin.

Jo turned around to face Zarina.

"I really enjoyed my time with her," said Jo. "I'm still enjoying it. She is so hot. I love her silky black hair and her perfect caramel skin, and how responsive her body is to my every touch."

As she spoke, Jo ran the tips of her fingers gently along Zarina's belly, watching her nipples as they jutted immediately into rosy peaks. She felt Kevin's hot bulge on the back of her purple leather booty shorts and she pressed appreciatively against it, lowering her head to run her tongue along the center of Zarina's abdomen, first to one breast, lingering to take it into her mouth, then the other, squeezing the alternate nipple with her fingers as Zarina moaned with pleasure, her head back. Jo was panting herself, as Kevin's two strong fingers had found their way around her right thigh and into the opening in her booty shorts and her wet, burning need. She rolled her hips against his fingers in a steady rhythm. His rhythm matched hers as he squeezed his ass and ground his rock-hard erection against her perfect curves inside the slick, cool leather of her purple shorts.

Jo brought her fingers down Zarina's abdomen and

between Zarina's legs, feeling the softness, the heat, the ache, as Zarina arched against the restraints.

"I need a better angle," said Jo, walking around toward the end of the bed, first stopping to take two things from the wall. It was a black and red feather duster with a leather handle, and something else. Zarina watched as Jo returned to the bottom of the bed, where Kevin was waiting. Jo used the feather duster to gently sweep across the insides of Zarina's spread legs, her belly, her nipples. The sensation was amazing, and Zarina's entire body responded by breaking out in goose bumps. Jo bent at the waist, lowering her head and darting her tongue around the sensitive skin on the insides of Zarina's thighs as Zarina watched. Kevin returned to his position behind Jo, now placing his hands firmly on her upper thighs, making the opening in her shorts wider and using his tongue to arouse her. She widened her stance to allow this, continuing her oral pleasure of Zarina, one hand on the iron bed frame to steady herself, her right hand using the feather duster to flick across Zarina's nipples.

Zarina and Jo both sighed and groaned in response to the intense oral pleasure they were receiving.

"Fuck me, Kevin," ordered Jo. She climbed onto the bed onto all fours, picking up the other item she had retrieved from the wall: a very realistic vibrating dildo. She looked at Zarina, smiling, holding it up to her for approval. Zarina nodded her approval enthusiastically.

"Hell yes, Empress Josephine," Zarina responded.

Kevin was also happy to do as he was told. He climbed onto the bed behind Jo, first letting himself feel the curve of her ass with his rigid shaft. As Zarina watched, Jo moistened the head of the vibrator with her mouth then switched on the finely detailed, ridged, flesh-toned dildo to the setting she wanted. The tiny pearls inside its head vibrated as the shaft made small circular motions. She placed it gently to the tip of Zarina's clit with her right hand, leaning her head down to take her left nipple into her mouth and arching her back toward Kevin. He thrust into her with a loud groan as he entered the velvety softness of her soft cave. Jo contracted her muscles around his throbbing dick, feeling every inch of his desire, contained for so long.

The three moved in harmony, Zarina rolling her hips to create more force against the vibrating head of the dildo, willing Jo to press it into her further. Jo teased her with it, slipping it just inside, back out, inside, out, while Kevin did the same to her. She rolled her hips backward but after his initial thrust he had pulled back and was now teasing her with his length, allowing only slow movements. His hand was on her clit as he expertly rolled his fingers around it, taking the rare opportunity to be in charge of her pleasure. With his hands free, he could squeeze and tease her nipples, pull her hips closer to him... anything he wanted. Jo was breathing heavily... she knew she wouldn't last long before she exploded in orgasm. Just seeing how hot Zarina was in front of her was massively exciting. She loved pleasuring her while getting pleasured herself.

Zarina wished she could touch Jo. She had never been in a sexual situation where she was receiving all the pleasure and giving nothing in return. She enjoyed every bit of everything that was happening to her. She willed herself to relax and enjoy it. Watching Jo's face as she bit her lip and closed her eyes, moving up and down as Kevin thrust into her was so damn hot. The view of Kevin fucking her was hot too—his perfect body, its muscular lines as it held her, his hands as they worked to please her, all of it was thrilling. She didn't feel like she was cheating Stanley. He could watch this movie, and would, and they would together, and it would be the hottest fucking thing ever. So she took a deep breath, relaxed, and let herself slide into a full state of pleasure.

Jo slid the vibrator further into Zarina, pressing her thumb against Zarina's clit in exactly the perfect counterpressure. She licked her left nipple, teasing it into a full peak with her teeth, sucking on it, until Zarina cried out in the most glorious, long, satisfied moan of orgasm, and relaxed beneath her touch.

Hearing Zarina's orgasm was hot for both Jo and Kevin. Jo had already been near orgasm. She removed the vibrator from Zarina and placed the head of it to her own clit, using her other gloved hand to squeeze her left nipple, hard, as Kevin grasped her hips and increased the frequency of his thrusts. She exploded in an orgasm that brought stars before her eyes, screaming out in pleasure and within seconds, Kevin grabbed her hips tightly, moaning loudly, and released himself, finally.

Chapter 11

Back in Keytown in the August heat, Zarina's husband, Stanley, served an iced skinny caramel latte to Tara with a smile, then returned to the text conversation on his phone.

Zarina: once u see it u will agree- omg hottest thing ever

Stanley: Rather just have u here. Never wanted to run Zoomdweebies alone ☹

Zarina: I knowww, sorry. Never meant to be on island so much

Stanley: I remember. "I just need to run the website from here..."

Zarina: Just didn't know we'd be doing so

much video…
Stanley: Didn't know you'd be IN video ;p

Zarina: lol me either but u r gonna need to trust me on that one…

Stanley: send it over!!

Zarina: the file is huge. I can upload it to a private YouTube video or burn it on a DVD and bring it home tonight.

Stanley: just do that and we can watch it in bed.

Zarina: Sounds like fun. holy shit BRB someone is knocking at the front door…

Zarina put down her phone just as Jo was walking into the room. They were both staring at the door, where they could hear someone, or what sounded like several people, knocking loudly on the door. Normally, people didn't knock on their locked front door, because they were expected, and everyone knew to use the side entrance, which had a key code.

"Where's Kevin?" whispered Zarina.

"He's already left," answered Jo.

She was still wearing the purple leather outfit. She grabbed a long black trench coat from the hook on the wall, quickly taking off the blond wig and pulling out bobby pins, trying to toss her black hair back into place. There wasn't time to change out of the platform heels. Zarina had changed back into the jeans and T-shirt she'd been wearing. Their cars were out front, so not answering the door didn't seem like an option.

Zarina waited by the door, looking at Jo for the signal it was OK to answer.

Jo shrugged her shoulders, waving her right hand toward the door. There was no filming going on. *Nothing to see here.*

Zarina unlocked the door.

Keytown Police Chief Christopher Linden, Matthew's Island Elementary School Principal Tony Spannek, and Talbot County Sheriff Gary Calderson walked into the small lobby area.

"Are you open for business?" asked the county sheriff with a smile and a nod of his hat to Zarina.

"Hello, boss," Jo said to the principal. "What brings you here?"

Principal Spannek looked down at the reception area magazines on the table, fixating his gaze on the latest issue of *Vogue* because seeing his kindergarten teacher staff member in a purple leather bustier would have been an incredibly awkward alternative.

Chief Linden answered for him.

"Hello, ladies," said Chief Linden. "Why don't we all have a seat?"

"I'm fine standing," said Jo. "Why don't you tell us what brings the three of you to our office on this fine day?"

"There have been some complaints," Chief Linden began. "And there is a bit of an investigation."

"Complaints?" Zarina asked in her tiniest voice. She was clearly terrified. She had served Chief Linden a medium coffee, black, two Splendas probably a hundred times back at Zoomdweebies in Keytown, and he now smiled at her sympathetically. "About noise or something? We don't really have any neighbors."

"No," said Sheriff Calderson, "it's not about the noise. Apparently some local folks seem to be of the mind that your business here is a bit unsavory and they have some concerns that it might be illegal. We've been asked to look into things."

Jo looked at her boss. "Are you a police investigator now?"

"The allegations about you," Principal Spannek began, his face red, not making eye contact, "about your, er — part-time work, I am concerned about how your kindergarten teaching position would be affected here in the community if the rumors were true…"

"So you came here because there are rumors on the island about me," said Jo. "Not because of any performance-related issues regarding my work, is that correct?"

Principal Spannek, whose head remained firmly down, had now memorized every headline on the cover of *Vogue,* and had learned that New York Rangers goalie Henrik Lundqvist, featured on the cover, was apparently the best-dressed NHL hockey player in the world.

"Well, there are people suggesting that your position could be compromised if…" he muttered.

"The place of business you are now standing in," began Jo, "is a video and web editing operation that I run part time. The hours I spend here, especially while it's summer and school isn't even in session, have never affected my position at the school. Many other teachers have part-time businesses on the side, especially in summer."

"In terms of the types of materials that are produced by the video production company," said Chief Linden, "and the website that's being run from both the Keytown jurisdiction as well as here at the Matthew's Island property, we really are just trying to ensure that all the laws are being followed."

"All the laws," said Jo. "OK, let's stop beating around the metaphorical and even the literal bush here. Are you gentlemen concerned about pornography?"

Two uniformed officers of the law and an elementary school principal dropped their heads at the same time as though a priest had told them to bow their heads and pray for God's blessing. No eye contact was made.

Sheriff Calderson was the first one brave enough to look up,

"Ma'am, it's our duty to ensure that no underage actors are being utilized in the performance of any… activities at this facility," said Calderson.

"Well that's a stretch," Jo laughed. "Because we don't have anyone here who is underage, which means you don't have any evidence that there is anyone here underage, which means the three of you are here barking up the wrong tree. None of you has a search warrant, which means you're all trespassing, though I'm willing to extend to you a welcome as my guest this one time on the property. Every filming activity that takes place here is covered under a tiny little thing called the first amendment of the Constitution, and I doubt anyone here wants to spend a bunch of money going to court to argue *that one*. The battle has already been fought and lost too many times. C'mon, boys, this community is conservative, but we aren't Southern Baptists. We're just not that far below the Mason-Dixon line for that. So unless you'd like a tour of the facility, which I'd be happy to take you on, I guess I don't have anything else to show you at the moment."

Zarina looked at Jo, at the way she had confidently let the trench coat casually fall open during her speech. The full view of her purple leather ensemble was now on display, the full power of not only her sexuality, but the power of her *dominance*, her attitude. She cocked one hip to the side, begging any single one of them to defy her.

"I still have concerns about—" began Principal Spannek, still staring at the Armani suit on the Rangers goalie.

"If you have concerns about my performance as an

elementary school teacher in my classroom," said Jo, "you can address them inside your building. But if my work here inside this building affects my employment in any way, you'll be addressing that with my attorney in court. Because I will sue the board of education for violating my first amendment rights to free speech if you fire me because I have another job that in no way affects my teaching."

"Zarina, you know everyone loves the coffee shop in Keytown," said Chief Linden. "There are just some old-fashioned folks and when they find out about this sort of thing, well, they get a bit flustered and they think something ought to be done."

"I guess so," said Zarina. "But I don't think we are doing anything wrong."

"Like I said, it's an investigation," said Chief Linden. "All that really means to us is that it's a bunch of paperwork. It doesn't mean we're going to be hauling anyone off to jail. It means we fill out forms, say we did our jobs and came down here and checked it out."

"That's right," said Sheriff Calderson. "We did due diligence. You don't have kids and farm animals chained to the wall, so you're not breaking any pornography laws. 'Nuff said."

Jo smiled at the sheriff.

"There, see?" she said. "That wasn't so painful, now was it?"

MAGGIE AND Wes sat at their usual table at Café Tokyo in Keytown, happy to be out of the summer heat.

"So what's new at the theatre this summer?" asked Maggie, after ordering her Bento box. "Anything exciting?"

"Oh, just the usual," said Wes. "We packed the houses with every single production of *Les Mis*, because of course Alfie was spectacular as Jean Valjean, I mean, Jesus Christ we had the theatre girls, and mostly boys, lined up in the alley for hours waiting to get their programs signed like it was Broadway, all night every night. He was thrilled."

"So great the whole thing sold out. And he was so amazing," said Maggie. "He really could have played the role on Broadway!"

"Oh well, if you could just do me a favor and not say that too loudly around him, that would be fantastic," said Wes with an eye roll, sipping his tea from the Japanese cup with no handles. "Because I think 24601 already has his own zip code, so he doesn't need any more props!"

"Well, I had a blast the nights I worked at the box office," said Maggie, "there's so much buzz at the theatre on nights like that."

"Oh, yeah, it's fantastic," said Wes. "Now we're getting ready for the kids to come in and do the summer theatre, so everyone brace yourselves for *Seussical the Musical*! There's no stopping it now!"

"Aw, I'm sure it will be cute," said Maggie.

"Well, that depends on who signed up for summer theatre, now doesn't it," said Wes, laughing. "We don't get to go out and choose! Now enough about my place. Let's talk about your wedding."

"I just want everything to be very simple," said Maggie. "I didn't want to spend a lot of money. I want everyone to have fun, dance, enjoy themselves. It's just about Dave and I standing in front of the people we love and recommitting to each other — it's just a nice weekend away at Sharps Island, it doesn't really need to be a major production."

"*Blah, blah*, still a wedding," said Wes. "*Clothes. Tell.* What are we wearing. The damn thing is like weeks away and I've heard *nothing*."

"I ended up finding this breezy vintage summer wedding dress," said Maggie. "It's not really formal. I love it though."

"Not enough detail, obviously," said Wes, putting down his chopsticks. "I mean it could be stunning, or it could be like Partridge Family–hideous. Tell me it's not a Karen Carpenter dress, Maggie. You didn't go full Carol Brady on me."

"Jesus Christ, Wes, have a little faith. I own a goddamn vintage clothing store," said Maggie. "No. I went online to a few of the shops I know from the vintage retailers' association I belong to—there's a Facebook page, and I asked, and everyone looked around for me and sent photos until I found one. It's from the thirties."

"OK, um, hello," said Wes. "First of all, *you* and social

media. So, news flash. Secondly, is it like a legit *flapper dress*?? I need to see a photo. *Photo please!*"

"Oh, for cryin' out loud, yes, it is, but it's not super fancy with the hanging beads everywhere, it's on the plainer side," said Maggie, taking out her phone to search for the photo. She showed Wes the picture of the sleeveless ivory dress with ruched bodice, descending front-to back hemline, and beaded lace detailing.

"It's absolutely stunning," said Wes, taking the phone with one hand and holding his hand to his mouth with the other. "Oh my God, I'm going to cry when I see you in it."

"Well, you can't do that," said Maggie, "because you're the maid of honor."

"The *what??*" said Wes. "*Stahhhp it.* Girl, don't joke about something like that."

"Of course I'm not joking," said Maggie. "My daughters will be beautiful bridesmaids. I love Eva and Lisa but I wouldn't choose between them. And you're my best friend. But I guess you're married so you can't be the 'maid' of honor and you'll have to be the matron of honor. You can't be the best man because Dave's brother will be there, but you can make up a title if you'd like."

"The gaytron of honor," said Wes. "Naturally."

Maggie laughed, nearly spitting out the tea she'd just sipped.

"Of course," she said. "The gaytron of honor."

EVA WALKED slowly on the beach alone. She missed Jo, who always used to walk the beach with her, but lately she had been so distracted by this video business she never seemed free to go sea glass hunting anymore. Eva didn't mind going alone, though bending down to pick up the glass at the near end of her pregnancy was a bit of a challenge. She really only bent from the knees for very special pieces these days!

She thought of Charles. He had been absolutely distraught at the news of her pregnancy. She'd tried writing to him, thinking she might be able to avoid a conversation, but he had phoned her right away.

"Eva, how could you do this to me?" he'd said. "You know I love you and I would have wanted for us to be a family. I would want to marry you and to raise this child! Why have you sent me this disgusting kit in the mail? You are obviously with another man now and he can raise your child! I don't want to speak of it again!"

He had been outraged. Contacting him after all the time that had gone by had been a terrible idea. She apologized over and over, trying to explain that she was so exhausted with the pregnancy, and distraught. But she knew it was really an exaggeration, that she'd avoided him for so long. The easy way out of finding out who the father of her baby was would have been for Charles to agree to the paternity test. That had clearly not worked out.

I will just stick to my original plan, thought Eva. *I will assume Nathan is the father. Nathan is going to raise this child as his own. DNA does not matter! It's not something I can change anyway.*

Why worry about it?

But she did worry. The attorney in her worried. What if Charles tried to claim paternal rights to the baby? Eva had been struggling with whether or not to tell Nathan of the possibility of Charles's paternity throughout the entire pregnancy. Every time they'd gone out for a sail she'd think *should I mention it?* But then the peacefulness of the wind and the water would take over and she just couldn't find a way to break the silence… and break his heart. She knew when the baby was born, she could do a cheek swab when Nathan was sleeping and send it in for DNA results if she couldn't let go of the paternity issue. But as she walked on the sandy shore, breathing in the salty, breezy air of the Chesapeake, she tried once again to forget.

She widened her stance, squatting awkwardly down and leaning to one side to scoop up a perfect piece of pale pink sea glass—such a rare shade. She could walk past the brown and white pieces, and maybe even green, but not a pink. This beautiful shade was too rare to pass by. She held it in her hand and turned it over. Looking out at the water, she wondered where it had come from: a plate or a glass, a vase or a serving bowl? How many people had once used the item, how many years ago? How many tides and storms did it spend out there, getting pounded by the waves until it finally came to rest here on the shore of this tiny island, lying on the sand, at peace?

It wasn't that different from her. It has imperfections, still, but it had stood the test of time—all the years of getting battered, tossed around, its sharp edges, smoothed out by time and stormy weather. And now, this island, this peaceful home. Looking again, though, she saw the dark, gray clouds on the horizon. Eva could tell when storms were coming. She'd been on this island since she was small, endured many great storms, knew when they were going to be bad. This storm they were calling for wasn't some passing tropical storm. She could feel the low-pressure system in the way the gravity pulled her baby, who even now rolled around low in her abdomen. She placed a hand below her abdomen, supporting the weight there. She tried to turn the red sea glass ring on her finger, but it wouldn't budge. It was firmly planted in place now by her swollen fingers. She smiled, loving the way Nathan had wanted to give her some gesture of his love for her without wanted her to panic too soon about commitment. It was perfect. Looking down, she realized the shape of the sea glass piece was really almost a perfect heart.

She thought of the way Nathan made love to her, even now, even the night before. Pregnancy had never stopped her from being passionate, though she'd had to look it up online and show him it was all right because he was terrified he'd hurt the baby. She threatened to drag him to the obstetrician's office and discuss it in front of the doctor if he wanted, and he had respectfully declined, looking mortified at that possibility. She swore it was only in the first trimester she didn't feel up to lovemaking. The rest of the time she was just as horny as she was at any other time of her life.

The baby kicked. She returned the pressure with her right hand, greeting the baby with a smile. "Hello, little one," said Eva. "I'm looking forward to meeting you."

She rolled the piece of pink sea glass over in her hand. There was nothing like holding a piece of perfectly wave-worn glass in your hand as a "worry stone" to transfer your anxiety away. Watching the gray storm clouds on the horizon growing closer, she turned to head back to the safety and warmth of her little cottage.

Chapter 12

At the small bridge tender's house, as Labor Day weekend arrived, Jerry Tilghman ran all the computer models again, though he knew they couldn't possibly have changed very much in the last thirty minutes. The meteorologists on the Baltimore and Washington television and radio stations, and God help us the damn Weather Channel, tended to report on one or two models. Jerry knew from his years working there that these stations were understaffed, underfunded, and under the gun to get weather news on the air, and in the case of a storm like this, they had to do it round the clock.

As a shortcut, they checked a computer forecast model or two, maybe a surface map, maybe not, maybe their favorite software that analyzed several forecast models, but it was an imperfect science, which is why school kids were often disappointed about snowfall forecasts. They might go to bed having been told by the TV weather reporter than six inches of snow were supposed to fall, and wake up disappointed to no snow and a school bus in the morning.

Jerry didn't like disappointment, and he didn't like surprises. He was a guy who sat in a small booth day after day, for twelve-hour shifts. A guy who had a lifetime's worth of knowledge and a lot of time on his hands. The personal weather forecasting system he'd developed specifically for Matthew's Island didn't get broadcast on any TV or radio station or blog. A handful of working watermen asked him about the weather so they might know whether to head out early or late for crabbing, and that was about it. But Jerry Tilghman knew exactly when a storm was coming, how much precipitation it would bring the island, what the wind speed was going to be, and, in the case of a hell of a storm like Hurricane Camilla was about to be, exactly how much devastation it would bring.

Watching the choppy whitecaps in front of him, he thought back to the history of the many storms that had ravaged the island in the past.

The watermen loved to regale newer island residents with tales about great storms of the Chesapeake Bay. Inevitably someone would bring up Hurricane Agnes from '72, when the Susquehanna River almost blew the dam and destroyed the bay entirely, and many say in fact had, as it dumped tons of silt across its bottom. Depending on how many generations their families went back, older watermen would talk about Hurricane Hazel in 1954 with its winds over 100 miles an hour, throwing boats around like toys and wrecking the crabbing industry for a whole season.

In the most recent memory of local watermen, hurricanes like Isabel in 2003 and Irene in 2001 had done the most serious damage to the island, sending some of their boats careening down neatly lined rows of docks and wiping them out, marooning other boats in the middle of roads, blowing out windows, and taking down small buildings. Harvests were once again affected, money was lost.

When storms came, transportation to and from the island could become a serious problem. The spot where the drawbridge met the island had once been nothing but marsh. That created an issue when a big storm came, because the water level rose there first, creating a huge pond where the cars were supposed to go when they got to the island. Waters often receded quickly, and if the storm came at low tide, it wasn't too harmful for travel. Luckily the larger storms in recent years had hit at a lower tide; there had been a swell at high tide, the islanders knew when they were coming and simply didn't cross the bridge when the time came, and all was well again at low tide. Standing water lasted for days on the island, but didn't stop any cars from crossing back to the mainland.

But as Jerry sat looking at his computer model, he shook his head. He ran the numbers again and again, because a hurricane was really nothing but math until it was right outside your door. *It's all fun and games until the big one comes straight up the bay*, he'd told Helen for so many years, and now he muttered the old familiar phrase to himself again. *I know, dear*, she would say, and she would knit away. He didn't know if she'd heard him or not, or if she had just humored the old man with her automatic answer. Thank God she'd never been around to see this hurricane when it did finally come; the storm he'd always feared. He'd spent a lifetime taking great pride in never being wrong about the weather, but for once Jerry actually hoped there was some way he was somehow incorrect.

Right now, as Jerry saw it, there was no stopping this one from being the worst storm on record to hit the island, and in fact the entire region. He stared at the software he'd worked so long to customize. He sent an email to the state, though he doubted they'd use his models when they relied on the "official" ones from the state and the Feds. The radar imagery showed the white swirling storm cloud coming directly up the gut of the Chesapeake Bay like no other storm in history ever had. It was the storm everyone had feared and many had prayed would never come. Jerry predicted that within twenty-four hours the island would be flooded on both the mainland and the island sides, the drawbridge resting uselessly in between, so that no one would be able to come or go. And that scenario was not what they were telling people on the news weather reports.

LABOR DAY weekend arrived and along with it, Hurricane Camilla. So the swirling white cloud forming out in the Atlantic on all the news weather maps, which had suddenly decided to turn and make a direct hit on Matthew's Island, officially had a name. She looked like she was going to be one bitch of a storm, that was for sure, but Ron and Dale had dealt with some bitches before.

Ron and Dale had worked for weeks to ensure everything would be perfect for what they'd secretly referred to as the BSW. Since Sharps Island Inn specialized in the most phenomenal gay weddings this side of Xanadu, the "Boring Straight Weddings" weren't always the most spectacular affairs in the world, but they'd become fond of Maggie and Dave and company, and thank *God* the couple at least came with a cast of fantastic common gay friends of theirs like Wes and Alfred. Also, Eva lived right across the pond from the inn's owners and they'd known and loved her mother. Her friend Jo certainly was the feisty one. Throw a dominatrix into the mix, and we have ourselves a party.

Situated at the southernmost tip of the island, the inn offered 360-degree views of the convergence of the Talbot River and the Chesapeake Bay. A narrow strip of land connected the circular-shaped property that sat atop high ground surrounded by rocks from the rest of Matthew's Island, creating sweeping vistas of the scenery from every window. Photo albums filled with happily married couples filled the historic mansion, decorated in rich fabrics, family antiques, and nautical charm. The broad front lawn held hammocks where hours could be lost watching sunrises, sunsets, or both, the perfect backdrop for not only the wedding photos, but the memories that would last forever.

"That was Jerry Tilghman on the phone," said Dale, "he said not to believe anything we're hearing on the Weather Channel. This storm has apparently become ten times worse than anyone is saying. He says he thinks our road is going to go out and that we should evacuate."

"Oh, whatever," said Ron, straightening his glasses and rolling his eyes. "What is he, the government? Everyone knows Mr. Bridgekeeper Chicken Little is always crying about the sky falling and almost every one of these sixty-five is already on this island. The Matthew's Island Inn is full, we are full, the island is at maximum capacity. It's not like anyone's going anywhere now."

"Well, an enormous tropical storm turning hurricane was the last thing we needed," said Dale, pushing aside his ever-present cap to scratch his bald head. "The tent company is pitching a fit. We can't fit sixty-five people in an 1840 house for a ceremony."

"Well, if the road is out, the people from Matthew's Island Inn won't make it here anyway. Besides, if they're all drunk enough we can fit everyone, baby," said Ron, winking. "As long as we don't run out of booze everything will be fine."

They stood on the back porch and watched the turbulent

Chesapeake Bay. The whitecaps rolled and the water swirled and crashed against the rocks as the Talbot River rushed down from the left of the property and the bay whirled in from the right. They'd watched many, many storms over the years. The wind could make it sound like the island was being torn completely apart, the thunder and lightning terrified anyone staying at the inn with their power over the sheer amount of open sky that blanketed the property, but although the waters had risen, they had always eventually receded and peace had been restored. The inn's owners had faith that history would repeat itself and that no matter how terrible a storm, the calm would eventually come again.

Upstairs in the beautifully appointed Patricia Bridal Suite at Sharps Island Inn, with its sweeping views of the Talbot River and the Chesapeake Bay, there was slightly less optimism.

"Just perfect," said Maggie. "We picked a hurricane on an island for all our friends and family to come celebrate our wedding with us."

"Everything's going to be fine," said Dave. "Maybe we don't have the best wedding photos at the moment. But like the photographer said, we can come back and get those anytime."

"Yeah, photos are the last thing on my mind," said Maggie. "I just want everyone to make it through our wedding weekend alive."

"See, there we go. Fantastic goals!" said Dave, laughing.

He took her into his arms. "You know we could call the whole thing off and have everyone head home to safety right now if you think it would be better."

"I know, and we've talked about it, but from everything we've seen, it's too late for that now, and then we are putting everyone in danger having everyone try to drive and fly home in the middle of a hurricane," said Maggie. "We have no idea whether this damn storm is going to turn at the last second and come up the bay or not. At this point we just have to hunker down with our friends and our family and just wait it out. With any luck by this time Monday, we're married and everyone is home safe and sound. Who cares about pretty wedding photos. Besides, we have cake one way or the other."

"No doubt we are going to be eating well in this storm," said Dave. "That's one way to look on the bright side. Cake!"

In fact, Chef Herman from Paul's Café had taken every precaution, ensuring that all the wedding food was already delivered and ready for preparation prior to the storm. He and a few staff members were on the property staying in one of the cabins at the inn with Ron and Dale so that they didn't have to worry about getting to and from the inn and running around in the middle of the storm. Every detail was in place, including the rainbow Smith Island cake.

"I've been thinking about something," said Maggie.

"What is it, sweetheart?" asked Dave, putting an arm around Maggie's waist and brushing an ever-stray auburn curl from her forehead.

"After this is all over, I've decided that I'm going to go visit my mother in Boston," said Maggie. She put her head down, hugging Dave.

Dave held her, pulling her close. "You've been thinking about this so much since that letter came."

"I can't stop thinking about it," said Maggie. "I could never forgive myself if she died and I never forgave *her*. That's all she really asked for. It isn't too much for a dying woman to ask for forgiveness."

"I think the visit will probably be something that will bring you just as much peace as it will bring her," said Dave.

WHEN CHARLES, *the head chef at the Plaza Hotel in New York City, received at his office Eva's letter and the "cheek swab DNA kit," he was shocked. He couldn't believe she would send him this shocking information and request him to respond to it in such a cold manner. They had been lovers for years, their affair in New York went far beyond this treatment. He had fallen in love with her. How dare she send him this in the mail? For him to find out that he might be the father of her baby in an envelope? He sat with his head in his hands for an hour, feeling a range of emotions he didn't even know he was capable of. Having lost his own wife to cancer so many years before and now in his fifties, he had never been a father. And now, in his hands was this — this kit that would determine whether he was to raise a child — his only child — with the woman he loved and thought of and missed every day.*

Eva. How he'd waited and longed to hear from her. He'd been so patient, understanding that the loss of her mother and her marriage had been so hard for her, that her sons had graduated from high school this summer — so many changes. So he had waited. Letting her heal, allowing her time to find peace in her own space on the island. And now, now he finds out that, nine months ago on her last trip to New York when they were together for the last time, this union may have resulted in a child?

His sadness turned to anger. She couldn't have come to New York to tell him this? She cared so little? Her feelings obviously did not match his. His dedication to her had been so pure, so complete.

There was only one thing to do now. Especially with the child on the way. He would go to her. He must see her face to face. He deserved an explanation as to why she would dare send him this cold package in the mail.

He picked up his phone and called his sous chef, who was very surprised to hear that for the first time, Charles would be leaving the Plaza in his charge. Charles made a second call to the valet, asking for his car, a vintage Mercedes, to be brought to the front. He checked his phone and saw that the 228-mile drive would take four hours and eighteen minutes. He drove nonstop in the downpour, his hands gripped on the steering wheel, determined to face Eva the very same day.

What Charles did not check was the weather. The closer he got to the island, the worse the weather became. He was so distracted by emotion, he paid little attention to the driving rains, the pummeling winds. Although "Flood Area" signs had been haphazardly placed by the state highway administration long before the danger had been realized, Charles ignored them as he approached the Choptank Narrows area just before the bridge, which had been raised by Jerry Tilghman to alert drivers to keep away from the flood area. The rushing waters of the Talbot River and the Chesapeake Bay had formed a deadly mix at high tide during Hurricane Camilla. Charles drove his car into what looked like a black puddle but in fact was a floodwater that carried his car away in a matter of seconds.

It would be weeks before his car and body were recovered from the bottom of the Talbot River and Eva would see his name in the local paper on a list of one of the many victims of Hurricane Camilla.

Chapter 13

"I know we should be heading to the main house soon because they want to board up the cabins," said Ben, "but it's so incredible to watch the storm."

The view from the Black Walnut cabin of Hurricane Camilla blowing in to Matthew's Island was unsurpassed, but the storm was growing more violent. Though they missed him, Ben and Lisa were glad Max was safe visiting Ben's parents for the weekend far inland.

"I know I should be getting over there to see if Maggie needs any help," said Lisa. "But it is kind of hard to look away. Once we go over to the main house, if the storm gets too bad we don't know when we'll be able to make it back over here." They had packed an overnight bag of essentials.

The sky was dark, and the fire in their fireplace was cozy. The sound of the wind whistling outside was broken once in a while by the sound of a breaking branch.

One whole wall of the cottage was made of windows

facing the Talbot River. It was far too stormy to stand on the screened porch facing the bay. Lisa and Ben each had a glass of wine and were sitting on the couch in front of the fire. They were reluctant to leave their cozy island sanctuary for the hustle and bustle of the scene in the main inn.

Ben turned to face her. "I guess we better go get our fine wedding outfits on," he said. Placing his wine glass down, he took her face in his hands. "But first…"

He gently kissed her.

She returned the kiss. Outside, the thunder rolled. The only light besides their fire was the occasional lightning strike. Lisa lit candles for their coffee table—the power was already flickering in and out and they had been warned about power outages on the island.

"I don't really even know if it's safe for us to walk over to the main house," Lisa said playfully, with a smile.

"You know what?" said Ben. "You're right. These are the early stages of a hurricane. Maybe we should stay here for safety's sake. We can't take any chances. Hurricane Camilla is a dangerous storm. We should seek shelter."

He stood, taking her hand. She stood in turn, following him to the bedroom. They didn't have much time, but the setting was so romantic—the howling wind, the crashing thunder, and the bursts of lightning in the sky.

She paused, gesturing toward the bathroom. She hadn't been prepared for this and did not have her diaphragm in. He knew why she stopped, but he pulled her toward him, wrapping her into his arms with a deep, searching kiss as the rain pounded the window beside them.

"This could be the end of the world," Ben said to Lisa. "Don't you think we should try to do our part in continuing the species?" He smiled at her, once again revealing the dimple that had been the very reason she'd fallen in love with him the first day he walked into her bakery to become the graphic designer for her new logo.

Lisa looked at him. This was serious territory. He knew she'd wanted a baby more than anything, for years. Hadn't been able to get pregnant with her first husband and had a miscarriage when she finally did. She wanted more than anything to be a mother. But her first thought was Max. He read her mind.

"Don't you think he'd be a great big brother?" Ben asked.

"Of course I do," said Lisa, kissing him, fighting back the emotion she felt swell to her heart.

He used his fingertips to graze across her breastbone and over her small, firm breasts. She wrapped her arms around his waist, pulling him closer, trying to fight off thoughts of being late for Maggie's wedding. *Maggie will understand*, she thought, smiling to herself.

Ben and Lisa made love with the great symphony of a storm as the backdrop. Their bodies met one another in time with the rhythms of the waves and the winds and the rain and the thunder, with the lighting of the changing gray skies and the great white lightning bolts.

As they lay together, holding one another, the driving rain pounding against the window, they made each other feel safe from the storm. Ben reached over to the small bedside table and took a small object from the drawer.

"I've loved you from the first moment I laid eyes on you," Ben told her, slipping a breathtaking, emerald-cut, platinum-set diamond onto her left ring finger, just as a huge bolt of lightning struck outside over the river, lighting up their room. She looked at him, his face lit with happiness. "Marry me."

"Oh, Ben. I will love you forever," said Lisa. "Nothing would make me happier than to be your wife. You have made me so happy already. Yes. *Yes*!"

"You're going to be an amazing mother," said Ben.

"I can't wait," said Lisa. "For our little family."

HURRICANE CAMILLA raged on in full force. Most of the wedding guests were trapped on the other side of the island at Matthew's Island Inn, unable to take the shuttle to Sharps Island Inn because the winds and the rains were too severe to even drive the three short miles across the island. Some had been evacuated. The road was flooded, and you couldn't see out a car window to make the short trip anyway.

The ceremony was supposed to have been outside on the lawn, with the reception in an enormous tent. The tent company had never made it anywhere near the island, turning back when the weather had become too bad. Maggie counted her blessings. The people closest to her, her husband-to-be (and former husband, if you were keeping track), her daughters, and best friends were all with her under this one roof. Yes, there were many others — distant relatives, business associates, and other friends from town who hadn't even made it through the storm far enough to get to the island and she prayed for their safety as well, but her world was here with her and it was all that mattered.

The guests had gathered in the sunroom of Sharps Island Inn, watching the lightning tear across the sky, the trees practically bent in half from the howling wind, and the waves crash over the tops of the high coastline. Dave and Maggie, Lisa and Ben were there, and Wes and Alfie, Eva and Nathan, Zarina and Stanley, and Jo and Kevin, who was more or less serving as Jo's date and had also volunteered to be the photographer since the original photographer hadn't been able to make it to the island.

They'd been spending their time in a nearby safer inside room, but knew this would be their last chance to see outside for a while.

"Enjoy your view for a few more minutes!" said Ron. "Nature is gorgeous when she's pissed but we can't let Camilla blow out the forty-six windows in this room." Ron and Dale helped as several of their staff prepared to board up the glass windows.

"Wait," said Dale. "Is there something we'd like to do first?" Having many years earlier become a reverend in order to perform ceremonies at the inn, Dale proposed that a brief wedding ceremony now be performed.

"I love the idea," said Maggie. "Let's get married in the middle of a hurricane, before it all goes to hell!"

"Why not?!" Dave agreed.

"Can you give me five minutes to change?" Maggie asked Ron.

"Well, that certainly will be a bridal record!" said Ron. "OK—off you go!"

Maggie and her daughters, Lilith and Erica, dashed up to the Patricia Bridal Suite (it was the inn's largest, with a sitting room where she could watch the bay if someone hadn't boarded up the windows already). Lilith and Erica changed in moments into the plain silk blush-colored dresses, chosen together at Maggie's shop, that had once been bridesmaids dresses from a wedding from a decade before. The dresses had only needed minor alterations, were inexpensive, and didn't look out of style.

The young women quickly helped their mother into her dress.

"Mom, you look gorgeous," said Erica, zipping the vintage thirties gown, seeing her mother's reflection in the vintage standing oval mirror.

"Thank you, honey," said Maggie.

"Oh, Mom, this is so exciting," said Lilith. "We're so happy for you and Dad."

"We have something for you," said Erica. She motioned to

her sister, who handed her a ring box.

"We had them restored," said Lilith, handing the box to Maggie. "We thought you might like to have them back."

Maggie opened the jeweler's box. Inside were her original wedding rings, the 18k gold half-carat round diamond and plain gold band. They'd been soldered into one ring and appeared as new as the day she'd received them, nearly thirty years before.

The rings brought back so many memories and emotions for Maggie, who struggled not to cry in front of her grown daughters. She took the rings, now one, from the box, and placed them on her right hand. She wore her new Tiffany diamond on her left hand and would receive its match at the ceremony today, but now she had the keepsake of all the memories from their years together raising their girls. This simpler piece of jewelry was a beautiful reminder of their family's early years together. She hugged her girls.

"Thank you, girls," said Maggie. "You both make me so proud and I love you both so much. I'm happy to wear this ring as a reminder of all the wonderful years raising you."

She wiped away the tears that had brimmed at the corners of her eyes.

"Now you're going to have to get me downstairs to this wedding before Hurricane Camilla rips this place apart," said Maggie.

"We love you too, Mom," said Erica.

"Glad you like the ring, Mom," said Lilith. "Now we have

to get this vintage fascinator on your head. Sit down for a sec!"

"I will fix up her makeup," said Erica, "while you do the bobby pins. We have a few minutes before we need to get down there."

"Nobody is going to start without the bride!" said Lilith.

"Well, you got that right!" said Maggie.

Downstairs, Ron tried to arrange the guests in anticipation of the bride's arrival.

"Let's all gather around the happy couple and make it quick!" said Ron, a bit worried about the safety of the guests in the glass room. "Thank heavens the dining room doesn't have very many windows, and also that we have a gas stove — so Chef Herman and his staff are in there right now making a fantastic feast for us to eat after this!"

Dave stood at the front of the room, next to Dale, who stood at a small podium and would perform the brief ceremony.

"The Lord will protect us here," said Dale, "and give us his blessings in this storm."

As the words left his mouth, the power suddenly went out. The island lost power even in a regular rainstorm, so Ron and Dale were ready with candles and soon the large windowsill around the perimeter of the room was aglow with light, enhanced by regular bolts of lightning from the storm outside.

"Very dramatic," said Eva. She ran a hand along the edge of her belly, ignoring the pains she swore she was feeling there. She'd been having contractions on and off all day but she'd had false labor pains for a week. This was no time for a trip to the hospital. Besides, she'd been to the doctor three days before and he'd told her she was zero percent dilated. She was nearly two weeks from her due date. She'd just been standing too long, that was all.

"I'll say it's dramatic," said Jo. "Are you feeling OK, Eva? You look a little tired. Do you want to sit?"

"No, no, I'm fine," said Eva, smiling. "The baby is just a little heavy, that's all." Nathan stood behind her so she could lean against him.

Thunder rolled outside and a large branch could be heard cracking and falling from a tree. Lisa and Ben looked at each other, concerned.

"Oh, found it!" Ron declared. "I never thought I would." He turned on a battery-powered CD player, and miraculously was able to play the opening strains of the wedding march.

Lilith and Erica had entered the room, each carrying a single rose. Maggie had insisted on very few flowers. She came down the steps of the Victorian inn carrying six blush-colored roses tied loosely with a vintage ribbon. The flowers didn't take away from her elaborately beaded 1930s headpiece set against her red curls, and her beautifully simple ivory flapper wedding gown. Smiling, she handed her flowers to the beaming Wes and took Dave's hand. Their daughters joined them on either side. Dale invited the other guests to have a seat in the comfortable chairs around the room.

Dale read from his vintage minister's book, used for

dozens of weddings at the inn.

"Love is patient and kind; Love is not jealous or boastful;

Love is not arrogant or rude; Love does not insist on its own way;

Love does not rejoice at wrong, but rejoices with the right.

Love bears all things, believes all things, hopes all things, endures all things.

Love never fails."

Dale then read, "Learning to love one other and to live together in harmony is one of the greatest challenges of marriage, but you have shown that you can do that in the past and now you will do that once again, and through the end of time. Dave and Maggie, I charge you both as you stand in the presence of your loved ones and family and the Almighty Spirit to remember that love alone is the foundation of a happy and enduring marriage, and from this day forward your lives together will be full of joy and peace."

"Please join hands and look into each other's eyes," continued Dale. "Do you, Dave, promise to live together with Maggie in marriage; to be her one true love, to comfort her and encourage her, to laugh with her and dream with her, and to care for her and grow old with her until the end of your days?"

"I do," said Dave.

"And do you, Maggie," asked Dale, "promise to live together with Dave in marriage; to be his one true love, to comfort him and encourage him, to laugh with him and dream with him, and to care for him and grow old with him until the end of your days?

"I do," said Maggie.

"Are there rings?" asked Dale.

Lilith and Erica each opened a ring box and presented the boxes to Dale.

"May these rings before us," said Dale, "always bring you love and happiness. These rings are symbols of eternity and the unbroken circle of love. Love freely given has no beginning and no end. Today you have chosen to exchange rings as a sign of your love for each other, and as a seal of the promises you make this day. We ask the almighty to bless these rings and the union of your souls."

Dale continued, "Dave and Maggie, as you place these rings on one another, so does your love encircle your hearts. May these rings forever symbolize your growing love for one another. Repeat after me to one another at the same time: 'With this ring, I give you my heart. From now through forever, your heart is my home, and you will never walk alone.'"

Dave and Maggie looked into each other eyes and declared, "With this ring, I give you my heart. From now through forever, your heart is my home, and you will never walk alone."

Dave leaned down to kiss Maggie as everyone began to clap.

"Well, I was going to say that you may now kiss the..." Dale jokingly began.

"*Aaahhhh!*" screamed Eva.

She doubled over in pain. Her water had broken. She panted heavily as the contraction passed.

"I'm so sorry, Maggie," said Eva. "I tried to wait until the—"

"Oh my God, Eva, you don't need to apologize for having a baby during my wedding," said Maggie, "especially during a hurricane on Labor Day!"

"Holy shit," said Nathan, whose face had lost all color. "We need to get you to the hosp…"

"We can't get anywhere," said Ron. "Our road is out."

"Your road?" asked Lisa. "What do you mean?"

"I didn't say anything about it because I didn't want to upset anyone earlier, but in storms like this…" Ron began.

"We can't leave the inn," Dale completed his sentence.

"We have to get her out of here!" yelled Nathan.

Chapter 14

J erry Tilghman had never seen anything close to the likes of Hurricane Camilla. The thunder boomed, shaking the tiny building. A storm of this magnitude was off the charts. *Forget* the charts, and the calculations and models and the software he'd spent years perfecting. There were only the windows now if he wanted to see what this storm looked like. He could barely even see anything through those windows, either. It had been over three hours since the state of Maryland had ordered the evacuation of Matthew's Island. Jerry knew most of the people from the island were gone, but not all of them. Lifelong watermen and their families didn't leave the island—first, because they were faithful people who didn't believe anything truly bad would ever happen to the island, and secondly, because they didn't have anywhere else to go. These were their homes, and they couldn't afford to leave them or their boats behind. They also had an unfortunate tendency to believe that weather reports, even if anyone had ever paid any attention to them, which most of the island folks didn't, were overrated.

He'd already heard one distress call from a boat on the radio, the *Lady Sandy*, and heard from the Coast Guard there had been two casualties, Rachel Tisler and Tyler Smith, who'd apparently tried to flee the island on a small waterman's boat. The boat was found, capsized, but the occupants, who drowned, hadn't even been wearing lifejackets and were only found because it was earlier on in the storm. There had also been several cars washed out trying to get to the island from the mainland—no telling when those cars would be found. Jerry's emergency radio had stopped working about an hour ago.

"This is going to get a helluva lot worse before it gets better," Jerry muttered to himself as lightning lit the entire sky again and rain sheeted against the window. Jerry saw the small leak on the one corner of the building start—the one that only leaked when the rain came in straight sideways. The bridge tender's house was running on a small generator, having lost power. The drawbridge itself could still be raised and lowered at the moment, though it only had about six hours of power in it before that went out also. His plan was to stay at his post. He figured he couldn't leave anyway. The road was flooded out on both sides.

Jerry didn't like to think of himself as being trapped. He preferred to think he was in the best spot there was, the high ground. The storm could only last for so long, and there wasn't a higher place to be on the island — except for maybe up at the Sharps Island Inn. Those folks should be safe, Jerry figured, though they had problems of their own. When their road washed out like it had, they became their own little island up there. Sure, the founding family of Matthew's Island built its first house out there for a reason — because it was the highest ground. But to get to it, you had to take the only main road there was on this island. And just before you reached the driveway to the inn, that road got very narrow. In fact, at one point on the road, if you stopped your car, you could turn your head to the left and see the Talbot River, and turn your head to the right and see the Chesapeake Bay, just like Jerry could do right here at the Choptank Narrows.

What that meant in a hurricane was that when the water rose, and especially when it rose at high tide, those two bodies of water, well, they got together. Jerry scratched his head now, imagining what the island would look like at the moment if he was in an airplane. The piece of land where Sharps Island Inn was perched would appear to be a little island all to itself. And what was it that fella had said? *A wedding.* Jerry wondered if those folks even knew the spot they were in. No boats could get in there to get to them now during this storm, and no cars, either. He'd tried to get them to evacuate when he could, when the state had first started giving the warnings, before their road had gone out.

Drip, drip-drip, drip, went that leak from the corner of the roof, and finally Jerry grabbed a bucket from the small closet beside the door and stuck it under the leaky roof.

From that airplane view, the center part of the island would be its own island. No one could come or go from it right now, and boats would be seen swarming all around it, torn from their moorings and floating around like those loose plastic ducks in a kiddie swimming pool at the county fair — the ones with numbers on the bottom that swirl around and around; the kids pick them up to win a prize. Jerry was cut right off from all of that, too, at the moment. He and his bridge would just appear from the sky almost like their own little odd-shaped vessel unto themselves: a man and his bridge.

"I hope those folks at Matthew's Island Inn and Sharps Island Inn are all right," said Jerry to himself. He had long ago developed the habit of talking to himself, especially in terrible storms. He didn't even know he was doing it. Nervous habit. "'Course they don't even really know what they're in for, they couldn't leave now even if they wanted to. They're all just hunkered down at both those places at this point, waiting the whole thing out. Probably for the best."

He paced around the room, because that was really all the bridge tender's house amounted to, besides the bathroom. He wondered how high the water was. He knew from the tide chart that high tide was about an hour away. That was good, it meant eventually the tide would be going back down, and if this hellcat of a storm could just turn back, maybe things could just settle down a bit around here. He sat back down in his spinning office-style chair, deciding he'd try the radio again.

"*Mayday, mayday, mayday,*" Jerry said once again into Channel 16 of his battery-powered VHF radio. "*This is the Choptank Narrows bridge tender, Choptank Narrows bridge tender, Choptank Narrows bridge tender.*" He used the Coast Guard standard policy of repeating everything in threes, but yet again there was no response at the other end of the line, though he heard crackling, so he hoped again that it was someone trying to respond. He didn't know if the channel was overwhelmed with emergencies right now, or whether his messages weren't getting through. He'd heard the radio cackle to life a few times on its own, but nothing clear had come through. Each time, he'd dashed over to the radio to signal his presence, with no luck. He changed the batteries on the radio, just to be sure any messages could get through, figuring he'd try again to radio for help in a bit and let the Coast Guard know he was stranded. All cell service, not great in the first place, was of course out to the island. He had literally no way of communicating with anyone at this point. Thing was, the state had told him to evacuate, and he hadn't done it, so he felt bad calling for rescue and making himself someone else's problem in the middle of a hurricane.

Jerry thought of Helen now, looking at the small, framed photo he kept at the corner of the cluttered work area, covered as it was now with maps, printed storm model forecasts, and data. Normally his work area was tidy and organized, but he'd tried so hard to make some logical sense of this storm, to use his lifelong meteorological experience to "science away" the cold, hard facts of the storm. He hadn't been able to save Helen from the cancer. He hoped somehow he'd be able to help the people of the island to survive this storm. He'd called every house he knew, trying to convince the islanders he knew wouldn't listen to the evacuation warnings to leave. He knew none of them had listened, because he would have been able to watch them cross the bridge. Newcomers to the island had — the folks who had retired here from other places. They had kids and grandkids on the mainland and weren't about to risk not being able to see them again. They'd packed up a few days' worth of clothes quick as could be and headed over that bridge as soon as they'd heard "possible category four hurricane" on the news and long before that.

The "come-here's" they called them. *They called* us, Jerry thought, with a smile, thinking back to the time he and Helen had moved to the island, all those years ago. Among other things. "Chicken-neckers," "weekenders," "up-the-roaders" — there were any number of nicknames for folks who weren't born and bred on the island, and lived in the Matthews-on-Talbot community of new houses overlooking the river. Everyone got along all right, Jerry supposed, for the most part. Sure, there was some bickering. Some of the watermen didn't like their lifestyle being turned into museums right in front of them while they were still living it, others appreciated the fact that the new folks brought money and ideas and rip-rap that saved the island from being washed out years before.

Not all the people who were new to the island had the best ideas, either. Some were selfish and greedy, and didn't give a lick about the history or the environment. They'd wreck the shoreline and build two-million-dollar houses like the whole island was a game of Monopoly. If you were up in that airplane watching now, those cookie cutter monstrosity tax write-offs would be the first ones to blow right into the drink in Hurricane Camilla, just like the old Three Little Pigs story used to say. Money had been wasted on environmental studies and "shoreline protection" that had flattened the coastline and invited the full fury of the Chesapeake Bay right up the middle of the island, cutting it in half during Hurricane Camilla. *Huffin and puffin* indeed, thought Jerry.

Around the island now, most folks were on the second floors of their houses, photographs and albums from the first floors had been quickly thrown into boxes and brought to safety. Those who lived in one-story houses were on the second floors of their neighbors' houses. No one knew how high the water would rise.

In the photo on the desk, Helen was looking up from her knitting, smiling at him, an almost half-smirk on her face as if to say *get this damn photo over with!* "Oh come now, Helen," he'd said, "I just need a photo for the bridge tender's house, something to remind me of you on all those twelve-hour shifts!" And he smiled back at her now.

The mass exodus across the drawbridge had been a steady pace as those up-the-roader folks made their way right quickly up the road to safety and to their loved ones. But for the lifelong islanders (and oddly, Jerry thought, just for that crew over at the Sharps Island Inn, who seemed to be digging in their heels up there), there was no telling them to get out. They were staying put. Just like Jerry. A one-man island. In between the hardest downpours now Jerry didn't like to look out the window. He knew there was no place to put the black paint line underneath the bridge to measure that flood line now. The high tide had made it just about to the top of the road now. Jerry knew if he opened the front door, he'd be able to see that it wouldn't be long before water would start pouring right on in.

The radio cackled to life again and Jerry turned the volume all the way up.

"... **Coast Guard....** raise ... bridge immediate.... **Repeat... ... ...**dge imme...tely.... Barge... loose... moorings .... Direct.... narrows.... you copy? .... peat.... raise brid...."

Jerry's heart froze, but he got enough of the message to do as he was told. He immediately slammed his hand down on the green button to raise the drawbridge. He knew there was barely enough power left in the generator to raise the bridge. In his decades working there, he'd never once been called by the Coast Guard and been told to raise the bridge. A *loose barge*? Was that possible? It had happened at the Chesapeake Bay Bridge Tunnel, at the C&D Canal, but never here. Anything was possible in a hurricane.

Jerry breathed a sigh of relief as he heard the familiar

sounds of the warning bells: the drawbridge was rising.

Clank-clank-clank.

Dimly, reflected through the sheeting rain against the windowpanes, he could see that the red and green lights on the bridge were working, not that there was any street traffic to stop out there.

But Jerry was a numbers guy, and as the bridge went up, he did the math. Those massive barges that drifted by on the Chesapeake Bay never came near the tiny Choptank Narrows, much less had one ever tried to make a crossing here. The barges, making their way to and from the port at Baltimore, were filled with enormous loads of cargo—steel, rocks, logs, electronics, you name it. They were half a football field long or longer, and they carried a ton or more of goods. Far too heavy to be tossed around in a storm like this, they were normally moored down in the Chesapeake until it was their turn to be brought by their tugboats into port. Why, the only way one of them could break free, come this way and do any harm in a storm like this, would be if the huge, boxlike metal vessel was… Jerry had paused for a minute to think about it, and the horror crossed his face at the realization… *empty.*

As soon as Jerry thought the word, the sense of doom came down on him, and he let out a breath. At first it sounded like the booming thunder he'd grown used to hearing for hours now in the distance, getting louder as it came closer. But he knew that wasn't what he was hearing this time. And he knew there wasn't anything he could do to stop this final ship as it sailed through his narrows. He had opened the bridge for its last time. The darkness, he thought, had been complete that night, but the depths of the blackness got far deeper as he looked up to see the massive shadow of the twisted heap of rusted steel raging toward the drawbridge and the safety of Jerry's tower. With one final glance down at the smiling face of his wife, as though for reassurance, for only a moment did Jerry hear the bomb-like explosion, heard for nearly twenty miles around, of two tons of steel crashing through the 120-mile-an-hour winds into the concrete barrier of the Choptank Narrows Bridge, turning his entire small island into a gnarled, useless pile of debris in seconds, and almost instantaneously Jerry heard nothing.

There was no longer a link from Matthew's Island to the rest of the world.

Chapter 15

"What the hell was that explosion?" asked Ben. "I have never heard anything like that."

"That didn't sound good," said Nathan. "It's louder than anything I've ever heard on the island."

"We have to get her out of this room," said Maggie. "It's not safe in here."

"They're going to have that room ready in just a minute or two," said Dave. "They just wanted to make sure everything was really clean. And someone is in there boarding up that window now."

"Mom, I can't get a phone signal to Google it but don't we need to boil some water and get some clean towels and..." began Lilith.

"Yes," said Maggie. "Good, you and your sister get together some clean linens for the bed, towels, the sharpest scissors you can find, and some very strong, thin string and bring it to the room for her as soon as you can."

A window from a third-floor attic room could be heard exploding inward.

"We've got to get everyone out of this room *now*," said Ron.

Ron and Dale kicked into high gear. Ron directed their small staff to finish boarding up the sunroom, with help from Kevin and Ben, then quickly went to the kitchen with Lilith to prepare the boiling water for the sterile linens. Dale went to help Erica clear space in the first-floor bedroom that had been chosen to be used for the delivery because it had only one window (now boarded up) far away from the bed. Wes and Alfie brought candles from the sunroom to what was about to serve as the delivery room, placing them on dressers and window sills. It was going to be difficult to do a delivery without electricity, so every candle was brought. Maggie and Dave tried to help Nathan get Eva ready to move.

Nathan said, "Eva, everything is going to be OK, we are just going to get you…"

"*AAAHHHH!*" screamed Eva. "Holy *faaaaaaachhhkkkkkkk..*"

"How many minutes was that since the last contraction?" asked Maggie. "We need to start timing them."

Ben chimed in. "I'll do it!" He opened the notes function of his iPhone and began jotting down the times, estimating the first squeal that had come from Eva at the beginning of the ceremony. He had been there for Max's birth and remembered this part of the drill.

Nathan took one of Eva's elbows and Maggie the other.

"OK, Eva, we need to walk you to the bedroom before the next contraction hits," said Nathan. "Let's go. You can do this. We are just going for a little walk. Just like on the beach."

"No sea glass today," said Jo, "but man, Eva, this hurricane is going to bring us all the good stuff."

"You know it," said Eva. "AHHHHHH SHHITTTTT!" She stopped in the doorway to the bedroom, doubled over by a contraction.

"You're almost there, kid," said Maggie. "Look, the bed's all ready for you."

Maggie and Nathan helped her into the bathroom and into a bathrobe.

Dave carried a soup pot of wrung-out clean, hot towels to the bedroom. At this point in the shuffling around, it was uncertain who would remain in the room until Eva suddenly took charge in between contractions. The attorney with years of experience slaying corporations in the courtroom wasn't thrilled about her lack of control over the current situation, but she'd keep as much of her dignity as she could.

"OK, listen up, everyone," Eva began, walking out of the bathroom in her robe. "I have to make this quick. I only want Nathan and Maggie and Lisa in this room. Everyone else can help by bringing them what we need. For instance, I need a goddamn bottle of wine, STAT if I am going to deliver a baby with no anesthesia. Keep it coming. And everyone can go dig through your purses because whoever has the best prescription painkiller better get that shit in here quick too. OK, everyone?

Let's do this… AAAAAHGGHH FUCCKKKK!!!!"

"We love you, Eva," said Lisa. She and Maggie helped Lisa into the bed. "You can do this."

"It's been a really long time," said Eva. "I do remember it hurts like a motherfucker."

"Like ridin' a bike, kid," said Maggie. "You'll be fine."

Lisa and Maggie stood at the head of the bed and held her hands so she could grip them if needed.

The room was cleared. An open bottle of wine, a glass, and a bottle of Ativan appeared within seconds. Under other circumstances the two might not have been prescribed medically to be taken together, but given the current set of conditions Eva took two pills and chased them with an entire glass of wine.

"I hope that takes the edge off, Eva," Nathan said. He was white as a sheet.

"Oh, honey," said Eva. She suddenly looked more worried about him than she did about herself. "Pour yourself some of that and take one of those pills. We're going to have a baby! Everything will be fine."

"Ben is outside and he's keeping the contraction times if we need them," said Lisa.

"Nathan, I'm going to need you to be strong, we can do this, don't pass out on me, said Eva. "I think we might be *AAAGHHHHGOODDAMMITT…*"

"Two minutes," said Ben from outside the door.

"Oh shit," said Maggie, holding a phone flashlight for

lighting. "Yeah, Nathan, you're going to need to take a look."

She helped fold the sheets so it would be easier to see, then took a look herself because he seemed to be a little bit in shock. Lisa asked if she wanted some water as well as the wine. She poured her another glass, handing it to her.

"No, just the wine for now is good, I can drink water after I have the baby with no drugs," said Eva, gulping. "I better at least have a good buzz going when I push this kid out."

"OK," said Nathan.

"OK?" said Maggie. "I'm going to keep holding the phone flashlight, because it's going to be the best lighting we have right now. Are you going to be OK?"

"Yes," said Nathan, forcing himself to stay focused. He looked at Eva; she could see him force a normal expression onto his face. He smiled. "You're doing great, honey. I love you."

Eva laughed. "I'm doing better than you. *AHHHHHHH FUCKKKKKKING HELLLLLLLLL!!!!!!!*"

She sat up, her face contorted. Lisa grabbed the empty wine glass.

"One minute," came Ben's voice from outside the door.

"Shit, honey, when you have a baby, you don't mess around," said Maggie. "This is hard and heavy. None of that seven-hour labor bullshit for you."

"Had the twins in forty-five minutes," said Eva, lying back, panting. Her black hair was covered in sweat, her face beet-red.

"Damn!" said Lisa, looking pale. She took a deep breath, feeling a bit light in the head. She needed to be here for her friend, and tried to concentrate on squeezing Eva's hand.

"It's the low-pressure system," said Nathan. "The hurricane. A lot of island women have gone into early labor in storms. I was born during a storm too."

"*AAAAAAGGGHHHHHH THE HEAD*! I CAN FEEL THE HEAD!!" screamed Eva. "I NEED TO PUSH!!" She sat up and bore down.

Nathan looked. He could see she was fully ready. Maggie joined him at the bottom of the bed, holding the phone light steady.

"You're fully dilated and crowning honey," said Maggie. "You're ready to push. *You can do this.*"

Lisa had never seen anyone have a baby, and having miscarried herself, and wanted a baby for so many years, it was an emotional scene for her. She held Eva's hand and stayed at the top of the bed, feeling a little ill.

Eva pushed and pushed, screamed and cursed.

Nathan's eyes were wide as the baby slid out. His hands cradled the baby as, face down, the head of curly black hair was revealed.

"It's OK, Nathan, you got this," said Maggie, "you can just place the baby right onto Eva's belly." Maggie grabbed one of the clean towels, checked with her pinky finger to see that the baby's mouth seemed clear, and was relieved to hear the baby's first cry. It was lying curled on its side, and she saw it was a girl. So did Nathan.

"She's a baby girl," said Nathan, covering the baby in the warm towel. "Our little baby girl."

Tears streamed down Eva's face. The baby's head bobbed, searching for her mother's breast. Nathan carefully lifted the baby inside her warm towel closer to Eva.

Lisa smiled at Maggie, who covered Eva with a blanket. Her daughters had collected string and sharp scissors and rubbing alcohol from the kitchen, so in a moment they would have Nathan prepare to cut the cord.

"She's so beautiful," said Lisa.

"Of course she is," said Maggie. "Just like her mother."

"Yes, exactly like her mother," said Nathan. "What will we name her?"

Eva looked at Maggie and Lisa, then down at her stunning red sea glass ring, then back at her beloved Nathan.

"I have this cool club I've been a member of for a long time," said Eva. "What do you think about the name Scarlet?"

"What a beautiful name," said Nathan.

The thunder outside boomed and the wind howled on as the hurricane pounded the inn around them, the waters drawing ever higher toward the house, unbeknownst to its guests, perched on the safety of the island's highest point.

"And maybe we should choose Camilla for the middle name, since we survived this hurricane during her birth," said Nathan.

"Scarlet Camilla," said Eva. "It's perfect. She is perfect."

Downstairs, a fire in the hearth, the rest of the guests gathered around eating Chef Herman's delicious crab cake meal while waiting for news. Rainbow Smith Island cake slices were cut and on plates, and perfect for not only a wedding celebration, but a baby's birth as well. Nathan went downstairs and made the birth announcement as the thunder rolled and the rain sheeted and the lightning lit his path. Small groups of friends and loved ones brought plates of food and cake and glasses of wine to the new mother and her friends, the Scarlet Letter Sisters.

Six hours later, a Coast Guard rescue helicopter would land on the front lawn of Sharps Island Inn, rescuing the group of weary hurricane survivors from what had become a very small island that day — they wouldn't know just how tiny until they saw it from the sky. Surrounded by so much chaos and love, and very closely by the combined waters of the Chesapeake Bay and the Talbot Rivers, they'd never really known the level of danger they were in. For those moments in time, even during the worst storm of the century, they had all they needed — the love of friends and family, and the celebration of new life.

THE END

ACKNOWLEDGEMENTS

To my publisher, Jason Pinter, at the amazing, uber-cool indie powerhouse that is Polis Books: thanks for making this trilogy a reality, and for the Grey Goose Dirty Martinis in New York that made me feel like a real author. *Thank you.*

To Myrsini Stephanides of Carol Mann Agency, thank you.

Thanks to Christine LePorte once again for your excellent copyediting skills on the book. You have yet again saved me from messing up stuff and I am very thankful for your efforts!

To author David Healey, for his fantastic book *Great Storms of the Chesapeake* as a reference source. I was writing my first novel *The Scarlet Letter Society* during the "Great Derecho of 2012" and was at The Tilghman Island Inn when the glass wall blew in during the storm, which I didn't know had an official name until I read your book. Thanks!

And to my friend HRH Alex, who sat next to me outside on the island in an Adirondack chair during that Great Derecho of 2012 because watching it was *so cool* and going inside to safety was boring—thanks for the NYC lodging during each of my book releases, and for your friendship!

To Zachary and Alex (*that reading!*) and Brahm and Charlie and all who have provided *g-inspiration* for my Wes and Alfie characters. How lucky, we women who have gay friends.

Special thanks to Bob and Tracy at Black Walnut Point

Inn, the *real* southernmost tip of the very *real* Tilghman Island, for providing the bucolic spot (complete with *fox porn*), where I broke all personal word count writing records, and the inspiration for the site of the big storm and the big gay rainbow Jell-O whipped cream pool fantasy scene that should become reality so I can pretty-please be invited.

To all my real-life Tilghman friends, Patricia and John, Sue and Jay, Henry and Scott, the lovely ladies of the Tilghman Island Book Club who have supported the book and been such perfect friends. Thanks to Willy Roe, for telling me storm stories. Thanks to Stuart and Nadine, for the best writing cottage on the island. Thanks to Knapps Narrows, for my unofficial kayaking ("don't die!") membership. Thanks to Lisa, as always, for my happy, sandy place.

To friends who have supported me by showing up at book signings: you know who you are. I love you with all my heart. It means the world to me to see your face there. I won't ever forget that you were there. *Thank you.*

To my sea glass friends: even though I've met you online, you are very real to me. (I have been fortunate to meet and become real-life friends with some of you!) I talk to you more each day than I do many of the real people in my real life. Sea glass hunting was my reward for hitting word counts on this book and all my books, and that's why there's sea glass in each book. Now that I've completed this trilogy of novels, I'm hoping to work on a beachcombing memoir in honor of the meaning that our hobby has in my life. Thank you all for your beautiful words and photographs and for making me feel less lonely in my writing career. My job and my hobby are both pretty isolating — meeting people from around the world through the #seaglass hashtag on Instagram or in Facebook groups has made that isolation disappear, and I am grateful for your friendship.

To Charlotte, for the music. WOW. A *mix tape*? Awesome beyond words. Thank you.

Thanks to friends who have written a book review, left a review on Amazon or Goodreads, or shared my book on social media. I can't thank you enough for spreading the love. I love you back. Thank you.

To Tracy, thanks for being my other-half Wildwood T-shirt bestie, Flyers-Rangers (please see book's shout out to your goalie, though) cheesesteak and fries, peanut butter jelly Delaware dinner, movie buddy, *real life not-just-Facebook* friend. *Go Flyers.*

Psychics are awesome. I'm lucky to have two. One I've never met, in England, Mesina of PsychicWhispers.com. She's amazing. I've talked to her for a decade and she's never been wrong. She's not just a psychic, she's a friend. My other psychic, Lori Wheeler, of Mystic Phenomenon, is also my friend, and lives in my town. Also never wrong, she has helped me at book signings as well, and I am grateful. These people are important to me because not long ago I lost my little sister, Beth, to suicide. My first book, *The Scarlet Letter Society*, is dedicated to her. Psychic mediums can help you stay in touch with a loved one who has crossed over, and Mesina and Lori, who both give me the exact same messages from Beth (*psychics are real*) help me remember that even when we lose a loved one who's very close to us, they are always still with us. Thank you, Mesina and Lori.

To Michael Whitehill, for your nautical and theatrical inspiration.

Liz: since first grade and forever, thanks for always being there for me. I love you.

To Russ Smith, publisher of Splice Today, even though I know you don't read this trashy crap, still, I'm here thanking you for making me a better writer and for only cutting out like 65% of the curse words in my weekly essays. Thanks for letting me be your website editor even though the title "Senior Editor" makes me feel like an AARP membership is far closer than it is.

To Kara, I mean, seriously, dude, are you even *looking* for your name back here, because I dedicated the *actual fucking book* to you. Soooooo. Just a little bit more of an acknowledgment than any other acknowledgment (hair twist).... But seriously. I have no words to thank you for your inspiration not only in vintage sports car navigation, but also in creative thought process spontaneity in a metallic chipped beef environment at the Centreville Truck Stop, without which none of this trilogy really ever could have occurred. When I said "writer's block," you said "seafood dominatrix" and I just ran with it. Also, you're one of the best friends I could have ever asked for in this life, *soooo there's that*. Thanks, Hermey. I love you.

Thanks to my fantastic siblings and Mom and Dad for your unending love and support. *Angry Birds war hero brother, you know who you are.*

Thanks to my squad: Bob, Sarah, Molly, Faith, Bobby. You're my heart, always. Thanks for your patience when I'm on the island like some kind of diva who can't write without a water view. I love you more than I could ever say, and always.

ABOUT THE AUTHOR

Mary T. McCarthy's 22-year journalism career includes Salon.com, *The Philadelphia Inquirer, Baltimore Sun, Washington Post,* and magazine editorial positions. She's currently Senior Editor at SpliceToday.com and is an Instructor for The Writer's Center (Bethesda, MD) and American University's L.E.A.P. continuing education program. *The Scarlet Letter Storm* is her third novel to complete the trilogy, it follows *The Scarlet Letter Scandal.* Her first novel, *The Scarlet Letter Society,* reached #4 on the Amazon.com Erotic Romance bestseller list, atop *Fifty Shades of Grey.* Mary lives with her family on Maryland's Eastern Shore, where she enjoys kayaking and sea glass hunting. Find her online at marytmccarthy.com, on Twitter @marymac, or on Instagram @marytmccarthy.